A Pig Named Orrenius &
Other Strange Tales

A Pig Named Orrenius & Other Strange Tales

Mario E. Martinez

ISBN-13: 9781547133772
ISBN-10: 1547133775

Table of Contents

*This collection is dedicated
to my wife.*

The universe is under no obligation
to make sense to you.

-Neil deGrasse Tyson

Jesus of Green Grit County, Texas

I.

Jesus Carvajal of Green Grit County died after a brief chase led by Sheriff O'Shea, who tried to serve Jesus with a warrant for unpaid parking tickets. As drunk as Jesus was, he didn't feel the impact of the telephone pole or his own ejection from the driver's seat into a fence. Not even the barbed wire that snapped and wrapped around his face registered, though the tines went so deep that not even Alan Wheaton, the local mortician, could pull them out.

But to Jesus, all of it wasn't real. Just some vague memory he couldn't be sure was really his. All that had any weight was the chase. The sound of Sheriff O'Shea's siren. The taste of warm Lone Star. When he closed his eyes while speeding down I-10, Jesus opened them to find he stood in the midst of a long line winding down into the mouth of a great cavern. It was shaped like a fish's mouth and an orange glow emanated from inside the dark shelf. Slowly, the line moved forward. Jesus looked at the people in line, some old, others young. A lot of them carried horrible wounds that peeked from beneath ragged clothes.

"Where am I?" Jesus said to himself. Though he was confused, Jesus felt compelled to move with the line. He tried to scratch his head, but pulled his arm back when he found a piece of barbed wire wrapped around his temples and cheeks. Though he tried to pull it out, the barbs were deeply set.

It took him a day to get close enough to the sign carved on the upper lip of the cavern, which read, "Hell – Misrepresented since 1317."

Another day passed before he was inside the cavern, a place of immeasurable size and depth. Jesus couldn't see the ceiling. When he looked up, there was but a dark and roiling ocean. He was seized with the horrid feeling that something was lingering just out of sight, something so vile that it could scare him into re-death. Yet, looking forward was no better. There, Jesus bore witness to a score of red creatures with empty eyes and shriveled wings plunging huge hooks into the people in line before tossing them in a pit too vast to comprehend. And all this was done under the direction of a small brown man in clean robes, who stood at a podium of bones as though he were the maitre'd at some bistro.

As the second day closed, Jesus made it to the front of the line. The fires beyond the gates burnt his nostrils and his open flesh, but as he waited for a great hook to impale him, the man at the podium put his hand out for Jesus to stop. The man said, "Gimme' a sec, guy," and turned to a black phone behind him. With the receiver to his ear, the robed man shouted, "What are you idiots doing down there?"

A muffled voice that sounded like the grumblings of the earth itself spoke on the other end.

"Don't use the bedroom voice with me, Lucille," the man said. "The sorters aren't moving anymore... No, no. They tossed a Tony Welch then just stopped... No, I haven't tried that... Why! Because it's moronic," the man said as he slid a cigar from beneath his sleeve. He pressed it to one of the embers littering the ground and blew a thick trail of smoke. "Fine, fine. It's worth a shot."

The man turned to the eyeless gatekeepers and said, "Would you please throw mister... Carvajal into the pit?" When they didn't move, the man uncovered the phone and said, "Lucy, they're staring at me like I just put a strap-on on my head... No, no, just see what the damn problem is... Yeah, get back to me."

Once the man hung up the phone, he leaned against the podium and eyed Jesus. "Give it a bit, buddy. You wouldn't think divine justice is complicated, but then you'd be wrong."

"You're *the* Saint Peter, aren't you?" Jesus asked. "The guy who kept pleading the fifth, right?"

The man took a drag from his cigar and pursed his lips. "Guilty as charged," St. Peter said.

"But, I thought you watched over… the other place," Jesus said.

"This decade, Luke's got it," St. Peter said, absently playing with the small set of keys attached to his robe. "They say it's all 'forgive and forget' up there, but don't let that fool you. Dip your balls in a wine barrel at a millennia party one time and they'll forgive you, forget the whole thing even. You just have to do the grunt work for a few years." St. Peter stopped and noted Jesus' beard, the barbed wire, and smiled. "Hey, anyone ever tell you you look like--"

The phone rang. St. Peter reached for it and said, "Talk to me, Lucille… Uh-huh, uh-huh… What do you mean 'at capacity'? Until when? You mean I've got to wait until people enter re-death? Are the glutton beasts full or— Shit, Lucille. I can't wait that long. I don't know what you *could* say, darling. Why not just send some to Limbo? Not like the babies take up all that much room… Fine, fine. I'll tell him." St. Peter hung up the phone and ran his fingers through his hair. "Look, Mr. Carvajal. Normally, you're grade A material for this place. But, we don't have the room."

"Don't have the room? Where the fuck am I going then?" Jesus asked.

"You see the back of the line," St. Peter said and pointed. "Get to the end and keep on walking."

"Where'll that take me?" Jesus asked.

"Don't really care, buddy," St. Peter said as blew smoke into Jesus' face. "But, don't worry, we've got your name on the list. When a spot opens up, we'll send a couple of our guys over to come get you."

Jesus shrugged and walked out of the cavern, past what seemed to be an endless line of people, into the gray unknown.

II.

Crazy Doris Johnson was the only one that missed Jesus Carvajal once they buried him. She was the only one at the funeral who wasn't there to spit on Jesus' grave or there just to relieve some of the small town boredom. Even during the eulogy, Lorenzo Giraldo raised his flask to toast Jesus' death, hoping it was a painful one since Jesus never paid his tab at the Live-Oak, Green Grit's only bar. Erik Lazan, his neighbor, laughed loud when the priest, Father Hawkshaw, said that Carvajal would be missed. And, once it was time to toss mementos into the grave, all that was thrown in were unpaid bills and a bag of rat shit. Not even Jesus' family came from wherever they'd moved to, wherever they went to get away from him.

Only Crazy Doris Johnson, fellow patron of the Live-Oak, sporadic lover in the bathroom stalls, and friend truly stood at his grave then. The rest of Green Grit swapped stories of Jesus' many failures and/or turned out because a Rangers' game was called off on account of rain.

Crazy Doris Johnson wept when they lowered Jesus into the ground. She waited for the vicious crowd to go and found the shade of an oak tree near Jesus' plot. Birds, picking at the food wrappers people tossed in with the casket, flew like cannon fire from the hole as the bulldozer flooded it with dirt.

On the second night, Doris poured a whole bottle of whiskey into the dirt and another down her throat. After screaming at the tombstone for reading Jesus Carniball, she vomited and passed out across the red dirt.

Doris earned a nickel bag off a trucker named Mahogany and took it to Jesus' gravesite along with two bottles of rum on the third night. She smoked most of the bag and drank most of the bottle, leaving the last of it for Jesus. Once night was full on, Doris took the untouched bottle and unscrewed the cap. "One last taste, old friend," Doris said. She turned the bottle over, spilling an unsteady stream of cheap rum onto the dirt. The mix of smoke and drink made her sway with the light breeze. Her smile was a sad one, mostly induced by three thin joints. But, they made her think of other things.

Even then, pouring the rum on muddy earth, she focused on the sound of the liquid leaving the bottle neck, the splashes, the look of the mud as though it bubbled, as though it drank. "Give me a sign, old buddy," Doris said, looking up at the sky. "Let me know it's okay."

She waited for a sound a coyote or an owl, even a bat would've done. But, nothing came.

With a sigh, Doris hung her head. "It's fine, Jesus. I'm just being a sentimental fool," she said. Then, a wiggling shape caught her eye. In the moonlight, they looked like worms standing up in the rum-mud, wriggling stiffly. Doris got on all fours to watch them and squealed when a little fourth one sprouted out. A fat fifth one came soon after. She reached out for them and once her fingertips touched their skin, they snapped taut. Doris yelped in surprise and struggled against the worms' pull.

She tugged with all her might, but the worms seemed rooted firmly in the ground. Doris twisted herself for better leverage, hoping she could somehow break free. As she did, Doris realized, it was not a group of worms on her. Worms were not joined together at their ends by some thick root. They didn't have bones and fingernails. With a shock of clarity, she realized it was a hand. And it was pulling her.

Doris screamed and yanked with the strength of terror, extracting the rest of the arm and shoulder. Feeling the night air, the arm let Doris go and flopped on the ground, clawing at a patch of dirt nearby. Doris didn't wait to see what unearthed itself, her mind full of old horror movies where the freshly dead rose up, possessed by some ancient evil. She ran as far as she could, stumbling over gravestones and the tiered plots.

A voice stopped her dead.

"Doris, you crazy bitch!" it said. "You trying to pull my arm out of the socket? And, leave it to you to pour that prissy shit all over me. Crème de Menthe, that's the stuff I liked. Not that pirate piss."

Doris didn't turn around at first. She told herself the weed was laced with something.

"Shit, Doris," it said. "You get me out this far just to leave me for the damn buzzards. Help me! Just watch the arm. Careful with it."

Doris caught sight of the barbed-wire in the moonlight. It was wrapped around a tattered face hidden in shadow, but even without clear light, Doris felt its face was an impatient one. She walked back to the grave, hesitating at first, but the closer she came to it, the surer she was that the person half-buried in dirt was Jesus. "How…," Doris said as she stood over the flailing body.

"Doris," Jesus said, righting himself. "I'd be happy to fucking tell you if there weren't two tons of earth pressing against my balls. Could you?" he asked, presenting his arms to her. She squatted, took hold of them, and pulled, slowly unearthing the rest of Jesus Carvajal. He stood beside her and tried to dust himself off, but his right arm hung at an odd angle and his head leaned almost completely on his left shoulder as if to compensate.

Off in the night, crows cawed. The noise seemed to startle Jesus.

"Jesus… you… you died… how…," Doris stammered.

"There weren't any vacancies," Jesus replied. "Now, let's go get us a drink. Don't want my first day back to get ruined on account of that two-dollar rum. And…those crows are freaking me out," he told her, unsure why they did.

III.

At the Live-Oak, Lorenzo Giraldo was giddy with the amount of business that night. It seemed all week everyone wanted to toast to the death of Jesus Carvajal. Every day, another citizen realized some aspect of their life was better without the drunk, the louse, the deadbeat. Even Father Hawkshaw didn't spring into one of his long sermons about loving our brothers despite their faults; instead, he sipped at his beer and smoked his pipe in the corner, listening.

It was during Alejandro Navares' toast to never having to bother with Jesus Carvajal again that Doris walked in with an odd look. Eyes open and clear as though she viewed another reality entirely, Doris walked up to Lorenzo and yanked down her shirt enough for one of her breasts to spill out. "Give me two beers," she demanded as she quickly pulled her shirt up.

"Shit, girl," Lorenzo said, reaching for two beers. "I'll give you the beers to keep those withered old things covered up."

Doris took one and gulped down half. "I'll be seeing you," she said.

"Off to hang with Jesus," Lorenzo said at her back.

Doris turned to a room of politely covered giggles and some outright laughter. "As a matter of fact," she hissed. "I am. He was my friend before he died. He's still my friend now."

"So, how's the piece of shit doing these days?" Erik Lazan yelled from behind the back of the bar. "Is it toasty enough for him?"

Doris sought him out with her eyes and, upon finding his bald head, said, "Why don't you ask him yourself?"

"Wouldn't waste the gas on that worthless creep," Bob Lost said to Penny, though it was loud enough for Doris to hear.

"Hey, don't worry, Bob," Doris said. "I'll just go get him." Crazy Doris Johnson left the Live-Oak's swirling atmosphere of crushing laughter, a sound so obnoxious it made her tremble.

"You need to take a shovel, *pendeja*," Alejandro crooned.

"What for?" Lorenzo said. "The ground probably spit him back out!"

"No, I had to claw my way out," Jesus shot back.

Under the shocked stares of twenty sets of eyes, Jesus Carvajal shambled up to the bar, his yellow eyes scanning the drinks half-emptied. He balanced himself with one arm and swiped a bourbon on the rocks, splashing it at his wired mouth. "Ain't Crème de Menthe, but I'll take it," Jesus said. He looked at the gawking faces and smirked. "What? Never seen a guy come back from the dead before?"

"It's a monster!" one of the patrons said.

Jesus scanned the room. "Fuck you, Trimble," he said. "And I still don't have the money I owe you."

"Then, what the fuck's going on, Jesus?" Lorenzo said. His hand inched toward the baseball bat he kept under the register.

"I died," Jesus said as he leaned forward. "Then... I came back, dumbass. What does it look like? Hey, where's Halliday? The bastard... putting me in a cardboard box painted up like oak."

"I get it!" Green Grit County's former runner-up for biggest drunk, Abe von Snowdon shouted and stood, splashing his beer onto Father Hawkshaw. "It's... it's... it's the Second Coming!" he yelled, happy that all the interventionists and church groups might now leave him to his lonely drinking. "Jesus came back to us! Jesus came back to us!"

"He is not the Son of God come to judge humanity!" Father Hawkshaw demanded. "I'll sit through my share, but that kind of--and excuse my language--*horseshit* doesn't fly with me, no matter how damn odd this is."

"How do you know I'm not, padre?" Jesus asked, dangling a broken finger at the priest.

"How the hell would you know?" Father Hawkshaw said. "You never set foot in church a day in your life."

"Didn't have to, padre," Jesus said, tapping his forehead. "Got it all up here. My daddy used to read the Bible to me when he was whooping my ass, so I got pretty damn familiar pretty damn quick. I'd say I know it as good as... the Father. Almost like I wrote it myself."

"'Take heed that no man deceive you. For many shall come in my name, saying, I am Christ,' so sayeth the Lord. To parade around these impressionable fools... If you dare say you are of the divine, then prove it," Father Hawkshaw said. "Do the work of Christ, *Jesus*. Let's see if your name ain't just an unfortunate coincidence."

"Ain't it about faith?" Jesus said, taking a beer from behind the bar.

"Can the shit, Jesus," Father Hawkshaw said. "You want to go around calling yourself the Great Shout and all, I need to prove to these buffoons that you ain't the Christ Child, just some freak of nature."

Outside, the crows cawed as though in laughter.

"Name the terms, padre," Jesus said with smiled with shattered teeth. "Because I'll take that bet."

IV.

The first test was the expulsion of a demon. Penny Chalmers' niece, Abigail Lintz, had a big one, so the town thought. She'd scream and howl for no reason, need to use the bathroom for hours, and as the days since her possession occurred, her skin seemed to thin and wrinkle. Already she'd stabbed a teacher in the hand with a pencil and was caught between the bus driver and a janitor in a horrid act. The girl even complained about things that weren't there; creatures, she said, like goats with squid faces, swam above her head, waiting for her to sleep so they could violate her. At their wit's end, Abigail's parents locked her in her room, where a strange smell emanated. Otherwise there was silence.

"So, do you think you can help that poor girl, Jesus?" Father Hawkshaw. "Or do you want to stop this silly charade? You never had much of a reputation to tarnish, anyway. One more act of cowardice won't harm you at all."

Jesus scoffed and started toward the house. Inside, it was typical of the residents of Green Grit. Photos of animals and faded family portraits surrounding a large television. Jesus didn't need to look far for Abigail's room. The door at the end of the hall was warped as though something big, much bigger than a teenage girl, tried to force its way out. To reinforce it, the Lintzes added three bolt-locks to it. Jesus threw the bolts back and opened the door to a room in tatters. Posters in ribbons hung on the wall and all the furniture was battered to kindling. In the corner, he found Abigail. She was a thin girl of sixteen with thin hair and wild eyes. Her cheeks looked cartoonishly freckled from where she'd picked at her skin. At the sight of Jesus sniffing the air, she hissed at him and brandished a chair leg like a club. Along the corners of her mouth were festering boils scabbed over. She hit him once, but only succeeded in sending bits of rot onto the wall.

"No need for the dramatics," Jesus told her as he looked around the room. He went to the set of drawers off against one of the walls and went through it, tossing underwear and glass pipes onto the ground. "Come on, Abbey," he said. "Just tell me where it is and we can get this over with quick."

"Where's what?" she said in a shaky voice, then threw her gaze to the ground as though something had scurried across it.

"The ice, Abbey," Jesus said. "The room fucking reeks. Or do I need to come over there and show you some of the mementos from my transition to the after-life?" he asked. He gripped both sides of the depression in his skull and pulled until the skin revealed cracked bone. "So, where is your stash?" he said, letting his scalp snap shut.

Abigail averted her eyes and pointed upward to a vent above her bed.

"That's a good girl," Jesus said as he pulled the vent out of the ceiling, which rained down bits of the plaster and clumps of dust. Taped to the duct was a small baggy with what appeared to be purple crystals and a glass pipe blackened by a torch. "Here we go," Jesus said, pocketing the baggy and pipe. "Now, you listen to me, little one. Stop picking at yourself and listen," he said as he sat near Abigail. "We've got to have a heart-to-heart."

"You're not going to tell me a young, pretty girl like myself shouldn't be spreading her legs and doing drugs and making my dipshit parents feel bad, are you?" Abigail asked. "Or that this podunk town cares for me or that my friends are all--"

"Damn, girl," Jesus said. "I'm beginning to think that janitor put his dick in your mouth just to shut you up. Look, girly, I don't give a shit about what you do. Want to burn the house down and tell your folks to go fuck themselves, who cares? I don't. All I know is that if you don't start acting right, I have to come back here. I don't want that--let's face it, you're not much to look at with that meth mouth--and *you* don't want that."

"Gross," Abigail sighed. She looked up at the ceiling, her eyes darting back and forth.

"Yeah," Jesus said. "Keep fucking up and I'll come back to show it to you." He stood and went for the door.

"What's in it for you?" Abigail asked.

"I wouldn't miss the chance to make Father Cock-Sock look like an ass," Jesus told her.

Before he left, Abigail called for him. "You know the crows are coming for you. They practically dance above your head."

Jesus looked back with such speed, his garish wounds wriggled on his face. But, seeing nothing, he left.

—◆—

Outside, Father Hawkshaw and the others waited patiently. Spotting Jesus, Father Hawkshaw stepped forward and cocked one of his bushy brows. "So, how goes the battle against evil? I trust it wasn't too difficult," the priest said.

"'Bout as difficult as falling asleep during one of your sermons, so I hear," Jesus Carvajal spat. "Didn't take a thing, really. A couple of slaps on the head and a prayer. I think she'll be all right. After all that, it feels like I got the icy fiend in my pocket."

"See, Father," Crazy Doris Johnson said. "He proved you wrong."

Father Hawkshaw glared at her from down his pointed nose and said, "Mrs. Johnson, in the seminary, I witnessed an exorcism. A minor imp was the culprit. The equivalent of a flea compared to most of Satan's minions. The entire ordeal took three days, and that was with a cardinal and two bishops assisting. I find it hard to believe that Mr. Carvajal, risen or not, could do the same in less than twenty minutes."

"When you're the real deal," Jesus said. "The rest comes natural. I'm sure they gave you guys some trouble, but I can mow them down easy. They know it, I know it," Jesus said and slipped a cigarette from his pocket and lit it between his shredded lips. "And, now, padre, *you* know it," Jesus said with smoky words that seemed to leak from his cheeks.

"I am not convinced," Father Hawkshaw said. He crossed his arms.

"Your faith is like a mustard seed, my son," Jesus said as he slowly exhaled an acrid cloud. Wisps of it slithered from his ruined body.

"Don't quote the Good Book, charlatan," Father Hawkshaw said.

"What, you want me to go make some wine?"

"Like anyone would want to see *that* face during a celebration of anything, let alone their nuptials," Father Hawkshaw snorted.

"They already have a seven-foot statue of a torture victim," Jesus Carvajal said. "At least they got my abs right," he said and pulled up his shirt. With one look at the bloated and greening flesh, Penny vomited on the lawn and Father Hawkshaw turned away. "So, what's next, padre? Want me to tell some stories about lost sons or something?"

"Let's just see how you do with the sick," Father Hawkshaw said.

V.

The next day, the crowd behind Jesus Carvajal swelled from Crazy Doris Johnson to Crazy Doris Johnson and Abe von Snowdon, both drunk and smiling. But, word spread about Abigail, who returned to school a changed girl and many detractors from the Live-Oak were there at the house of Jesse Flowers, the sick man Jesus was supposed to heal.

When Jesus walked into the house, with numerous eyes on him, he said to the crowd, "I'll have Jesse dancing the two-step in a minute, just you wait."

The house was a mess. Cockroaches scuttled from the light of the open door to hide under pizza boxes or behind baseboards left to rot. A thin layer of dust lay on everything. "Jesse!" Jesus called out. "Jesse, you gross bastard, you in here?"

"Go away," a voice said from deep within the house. "Go away. I don't want to see anyone."

"Not my problem," Jesus said and stepped in a dingy hall. The pictures that lined them were so covered in filth, they looked ancient. At the end of the hall was a door with the doorknob dangling like an eye. When he pushed the door open, Jesus scoffed at the sight inside.

Jesse Flowers sat in his bed, the comforter pulled around him like a cape. His full beard of scraggly hair peeked out of it, twitching with each breath. "Are you death? Have you come to…take me?" he asked when he saw Jesus. "Are you the one that's going to end my pain?"

Looking around the room, Jesus said, "No. No. And sort of." In the corner, an emaciated cat moaned in a pile of stained clothes.

"Sweet death, I thought you'd be a skeleton in robes… You're much uglier than I'd imagined," Jesse told him.

"And you're healthier than I'd heard," Jesus shot back. "Look, buddy, I need you to get out of bed. Not for long, just long enough to get the padre nice and riled up."

"What's the point?" Jesse sighed. "Deidra's gone. Gone!" He buried his face in his hands. "She'll be married and have kids and get old and she'll never know… never know how much I loved her."

"Man," Jesus scoffed. "Is that what this is all about? Some woman?"

"Not just *some* woman," Jesse cried. "She's what all women aspire to be. She is perfection… perfection I'll never have!" Jesse covered himself in his blanket and wept loudly, blowing his nose in the comforter and trembling like his dying cat.

"Why don't you just go see her," Jesus suggested. "And, when you do, just tell Father Hawkshaw that I did what modern medicine couldn't."

"I can't!" Jesse screamed. "I sold my truck to buy this ring," he said while searching inside the folds of the blanket. It was a small gold ring with a cloudy diamond set in it. "I was going to tell her, then… then, this happened," Jesse bellowed before producing a piece of newspaper from the blanket. It was a wedding announcement for Deidra Rosales and Markus

Delayny. "And, even if I could get out of bed, she lives in Sandstone. That's twenty miles away!"

"If I told you I could help," Jesus started, "would you do whatever I say? You know, have faith?"

"No," Jesse said, peeking at Jesus from beneath the blanket.

Jesus hissed, "What if I said I'd eat you starting with your feet if you didn't?"

"If I can't have her, you might as well. I don't care," Jesse said and slumped further onto the bed.

Jesus was surprised. So far, he appearance alone was enough to elicit some sort of reaction from people. The sight of a rotting corpse conversing with the locals would do that. If the sight of him couldn't do it, the smell of did. But, Jesse was unshakable in his misery. A sadness the likes of which could only be escaped, never overcome.

"You want to smoke some meth?" Jesus asked. "Can't make you feel any worse."

"What do I care?"

"That's the spirit," Jesus said as he reached into his pocket and brought out the pipe and baggy. He took a crystal from the bunch and put it in the pipe. "You got a lighter around here?" Jesus asked.

Jesse reached into the blanket and produced one.

Jesus lit it and put the pipe in Jesse's mouth. "Now, just breathe deep. Once this shit kicks in, you'll run over to Sandstone and scoop up that big Mexican peach."

Jesse tried but coughed once the smoke got to his throat. "It burns...," he painfully whispered.

"Everything good does," Jesus said, taking the pipe. With a body devoid of any sensation, the smoke was easy to take. But, Jesus also noticed that the familiar tingles that usual accompanied some good meth were no longer there. Rolling his eyes, Jesus burnt the crystal to cinders and held the smoke in his lungs. With one hand, Jesus pulled the blanket over Jesse as he exhaled the smoke.

At first, there was nothing but strained coughing from beneath the blanket. Then, it stood still like a cocoon shielding its contents from the world beyond. "I didn't just kill you, did I?" Jesus asked, reaching for a corner to pull back. But, the rumbling stopped him.

"I... I... I feel... uh... uh... amazing!" Jesse shouted, flinging the blanket off his back. Knick-knacks of all kinds fell and shattered from the open comforter and standing amongst the pile was Jesse Flowers, quivering with a renewed life, and, subsequently nude except for thick patches of body hair. "I just want to do everything at once! I want to clean! I want to love! I want more, more, more of that purple stuff! I need it! Oh, God! This is great, great, great!"

"Hey, Jess," Jesus said, putting his rotting fingers on the man's arm. The action engrossed Jesse nearly to the point of tears. "Why don't you go run to Deidra, now? But, before you do, tell Father Hacky-Sack out there that I cured you."

Jesse fell to his knees and kissed Jesus' fingers. "I'll sing your praises until my dying day!"

"Mind putting some pants on too?" Jesus asked, but Jesse was already gone, running out of his house down the road, gut and genitals jiggling with each step. He held the ring in front of him as though he would do so for the twenty mile trip to Deidra.

———◆———

When Jesus emerged from the house, his pocket full of the loose dollar bills left in plain view, the crowd was turned away, watching some speck in the distance. "When I heal 'em," Jesus chided, "I heal 'em."

The crowd looked at him with eyes wide. Yet, Father Hawkshaw scowled deeply. "Why did Mr. Flowers run down the road naked as the day he was born?" the priest asked.

Jesus thought a moment and smiled. "I told him now that I've come back," Jesus said, suddenly changing his pitch to a fatherly tone, "He need not be ashamed of his nakedness. Not in the sight of salvation." He spread his arms a bit as though delivering a sermon.

"Don't mock the Word, you bag of rot!" Father Hawkshaw spat, jabbing his thin finger at Jesus.

"Don't you talk to our Lord and Savior that way!" Abe von Snowdon shot back; the crowd murmured, some agreeing, others remaining silent.

"He's a fraud," Father Hawkshaw replied. "Some anomaly of science or circumstance. But, he is not the Son of God!"

"We are all the children of my Father," Jesus said and spread his arms out as much as the ruined flesh could. His right arm quivered and failed, making the sound of a tree branch breaking and swung in his shirt just as pathetically. Not to be deterred, he continued, "But, the doubters will always need their proof, my brothers and sisters--"

"Enough of this," Father Hawkshaw bellowed.

"What more would you ask of me," Jesus asked in a mocking tone. "I am merciful to the lambs that have strayed, no matter how much they run."

Father Hawkshaw sneered and said, "Fine. Tomorrow. I have another test for you, Mr. Carvajal--"

"Son of the Most High will do," Jesus said.

"We'll see," the priest said. "We'll see. Just go to the Veteran's Hall at six."

Jesus was about to say something, but then he noticed a small murder of crows glaring at him from the low branches of a willow tree. So, instead, he walked with Crazy Doris Johnson and Abe von Snowdon, unsure why the birds made him feel so afraid or why they followed his every step with their yellow eyes.

VI.

The Green Grit County Veteran's Hall was full by the time Jesus and Crazy Doris Johnson came in. Trailing them, a small knot of people, some nude as a sign of devotion to the Second Coming, all carrying Bibles and rosaries wrapped about their wrists, all talking about Jesus and his wonders. The hall was mostly wooden beams and sheet rock, where cracks and holes were covered up with photographs of the two citizens who died on Omaha Beach and a third who died when he fell asleep in bed with a cigar, a habit born in Korea. Round tables had been set up to the point where it was difficult to find room enough to walk.

Despite it, once Hawkshaw saw, and no doubt smelt, Jesus, the priest danced his way through the crowd. "Mr. Carvajal," he said as though he were relishing the moment. "I'm glad you could join us."

"I never keep my flock waiting," Jesus said, a smirk forcing itself on his rotting face. "But, what is going on? A dinner for Green Grit's prodigal son?"

"No," Father Hawkshaw said, smiling. "I was just hoping that you could... feed these five hundred people," the priest said, indicating the crowd with a sweep of his hand.

"I don't think my body would feed them all," Jesus said.

His followers chuckled and nodded as though the phrase led to salvation.

Father Hawkshaw motioned to someone in the crowd and said. "No, perhaps this will better explain it." A deacon in plain-clothes approached them with a basket and handed it over to the priest. "Here," the priest said, thrusting the basket at Jesus.

"What is it?" Crazy Doris Johnson asked. "Bet it's a big ol' snake 'er something. He's trying to trick you, buddy."

"Ms. Johnson," Father Hawkshaw huffed. "It is two fried catfish plates from the Crawdad and five loaves of Wonda Bread. I'd like Mr. Carvajal to distribute them and feed all the people here. Nothing more."

"That ain't enough," Doris blurted.

"Precisely," Father Hawkshaw said.

"If I do it, will you worship me?" Jesus asked in the tone of a boy hoping to ask a girl to dance.

"Let us cross that bridge when we get to it, shall we," Father Hawkshaw scoffed.

Jesus took the basket and looked inside it, then to the crowd. The faces turned and focused on him and the father. "I'll tell you this, padre," Jesus said as he walked to the seated people. "Ain't a damn one in here going to leave hungry. You all be sure to tell me when you're full."

Basket in hand, Jesus limped to the first table and put his dangling arm on the clean cloth with a wet sound. He leaned forward, letting his remaining hair dangle over the table. "Who wants to eat?" he asked and smiled, revealing his broken teeth and gleaming black gums. Jesus wiped a spot of drool and reached into the basket. He brought out a bit of catfish and presented it to the people. "Anyone? Anyone?" he asked, but, when they refused, Jesus could only smile. "Guess no one's hungry then."

When he turned away, one of the men gagged and vomited. Though some jumped at the sight, Father Hawkshaw told them to remain calm and stay seated. Others soon followed, shoving heads under tables and retching. A few couldn't stand the scene enough to stay inside the hall, bursting through the doors to vomit in the parking lot.

Jesus went to the next table and the next with a choir of dry heaves all around. Still, he offered slices of bread smeared with his grave-soiled hands, chunks of fried catfish from his broken fingers. All the while, he chose his words to breathe the stench of his decaying innards. "Hello and welcome, brothers and sisters. How good of you to arrive," he told one group who wore the stained faces of nausea.

Abigail Lintz--in a floral dress and braided hair in ribbons--sat with her aunt and forced a smile when Jesus came to offer her table some of the food. They declined a taste of any of it, sporadically heaving when Jesus asked about Abigail's progress. None of them could meet his sickly yellow eyes, but he clapped their shoulders and bid them salvation.

Only Abe von Snowdon ate half a catfish plate before turning to a box of dessert wine. The rest, Jesus gave to his followers. They ate the loaves and fried fish as though it was a sacrament. Their greasy fingers stained their leather Bibles and wooden rosary beads as they prayed in whispers, whispers to Jesus. When only a piece of crust was left, Jesus took it and offered it to Father Hawkshaw. "Are you hungry, padre?" he asked.

"No! You... you...," Father Hawkshaw stammered.

Jesus tried to pop the crust into his mouth, but succeeded only in getting it stuck in the barbed wire driven into his face. With a little effort, Jesus snagged the bread in his torn lips and ate it. "Well, I guess there's nothing left," Jesus said. "You going to call the bet? As you of all people would know, God will always forgive the doubters. I should know."

"No, no, no!" Father Hawkshaw spat.

"Not a soul here is hungry that wasn't offered," Jesus said. "And two catfish and some Wonda Bread was all it took. "

"No, I won't," Father Hawkshaw blurted. "So what if you rose from the dead! So what if you cured Abigail Lintz and Jesse Flowers! You did these things either out of spite or out of your own buffoonery! I will not believe you, pretender!"

"Well, what else could I do to prove it?" Jesus said. "And, that's pretty generous for the Almighty, I'll have you know."

"Oh my God! Help!" someone yelled from the crowd. "Mrs. Novak! She just fell over! It was all the puking! Call someone! Oh, my God! I think she's dead!"

Father Hawkshaw smiled and said, "Ask and ye shall receive."

Jesus looked at the people trying to revive old Mrs. Novak and mouthed, "Shit."

VII.

"No need to gawk at it if you can do nothing for it," Father Hawkshaw said triumphantly. He and Jesus stood over the body of Mrs. Novak, a bloated woman of seventy with dyed red hair and too much lipstick. She lay in the puddles of vomit--seven cans full by the janitor's count--that fermented in the stagnant air of the Veteran's Hall. When Jesus didn't move, Father Hawkshaw scoffed. "I suppose *this* is where your powers end. Not much of a Second Coming if you've no control over life and death."

Jesus stared down at the body and smiled. "Ye of little of faith," he chided before turning to his mass. "Guys, pick up Mrs. Novak here and take her to Doris' place."

"For what!" Father Hawkshaw blurted. "I'll not let you defile this woman for your own pleasures, wager or not. Take her to a funeral home so once this farce is over, we can put the poor woman in the ground."

"Relax, padre," Jesus said. "Leave her with me and in three days or less, I'll have her up and running. But, if it'll make you feel better, we'll take her to the funeral home. I'd think you of all people would have some faith in the divine. Even the first guy had his doubters, right?"

"I do," Father Hawkshaw spat. "Just not in the *rotten calf* standing before me."

Jesus swung his limp arm to land on Hawkshaw's shoulder. "Don't worry, I won't bring this up when you repent, my son."

Father Hawkshaw's face reddened and he jostled the putrid limb off his shoulder.

———————

Some of the men moved Mrs. Novak's corpse to the mortuary and left it in one of the viewing rooms with Jesus and Crazy Doris Johnson. Alan Wheaton gave them a blanket so Doris could sleep on one of the pews. Even with the doors of the small viewing room—a few pews and a podium on a wide dais—Jesus felt them out there. Green Grit. They peered in from the clear spots in the stained glass lining the room. Their whispers rattled the walls so that every voice rang with discordant gravity, a tangible weight Jesus felt in his dead chest.

But, no voice rang louder than Father Hawkshaw, who tried to claw his way to the front row of the multitude citing his religious station.

"So," Doris said, clapping her hands. "How's this whole bit work?"

Jesus shrugged as best his busted shoulders could manage. "Look, Doris, you know I've just been doing this to fuck with the padre," he told her as he forced himself near Mrs. Novak. He looked down at her bloated face, reddened and bulging from the exertion. "There's nothing I can do for the old gal."

"But... how the hell did you do it, then?" Doris asked, shipping a small flask of whiskey from the crotch of her jeans. "With all the excitement, I forgot to ask. Or... I was too drunk to ask. Hell, I don't know."

"Shit, Doris, take it easy," Jesus said. "I didn't do anything. I... died, I guess. Well, I *know*."

"And heaven let you come back!" Doris said in a mocking tone, toasting to him.

"Doris," Jesus scoffed. "You're something else. You know damn well I didn't see any pearly gates where I went. Just this… mouth. A line of people walking into the fires. It was fucking boring and you couldn't leave… You just stood there, waiting and waiting, but when it got to my time, it stopped. Saint Peter turned me--"

"Saint Peter!" Doris blurted, her nose crinkled. "Why'd he--"

"Something about piss in a punch bowl," Jesus said. "He just told me to go back and I did. But, who knows if ol' Wendy Novak here is going to be tossed to the fire or not. Maybe they fixed it, and some of us just got lucky. I can't say I remember a thing about that woman except for her walking that fat, ugly dog. For all we know, she's on her way to heaven right now."

"Naw," Doris said, lighting a cigarette. "I knew Wendy's brother's ex-girl-friend. She's going to *hell*. She told me Wendy used to tie up her dog in a tree-less yard, cooking that poor thing. Oh, and I think she used to beat her kids or something, I don't know."

"Well, I hope she beat them good," Jesus said. "If not, I'm just warning you, I'm going to skin her and make you wear her like a dress. There's no way I'm letting that son of a bitch get the better of me."

Doris stared at Jesus a moment. Shrugging, she laughed, "Done weirder, I guess."

———————

For three days, Jesus watched Doris drink and rant to herself until she fell asleep. He rotted in the shafts of sunlight pouring from the colored glass, maggots rising up through his bloated pores. He picked them out of his skin, looked at them, and crushed them between his fingers. Outside, the people quieted, though the devout kept their prayers constant. Occasionally, Jesus took some of the drink Doris and Abe von Snowdon brought in, but it sat in his foul guts until it finally leaked onto his lap.

In her drunken slumbers, Crazy Doris Johnson dreamt of Jesus Carvajal as he was, a lump of dead and tangled flesh. But, instead of rot, Jesus healed himself. The crown of wire pushed out and fell to the turbulent nothing of her dreams. Then the pockets of fetid innards became vibrant and hidden under a new layer of brown skin. And when she woke, she found the same loose skin and garish wounds but drank to the health of Jesus all the same.

———◆———

Father Hawkshaw had all but announced Jesus' failure as the sun set on the third day. "You see, my brethren," he said to them once the sun fell behind Nestor Palank's house behind the crowd. "This *Jesus* Carvajal is nothing but a fraud. A false prophet profiting from chance and coincidence. He's led you good people astray," he told those devout who still followed him. They only prayed harder. "He was quite the trickster, I'll admit. But, the one true God has shown true. His Son will not crawl up from the earth like a common slug as Jesus Carvajal did, but descend from the heavens. Look, even now the deceiver hides for he knows the time for the truth is now!" Father Hawkshaw said and pointed to the door of the mortuary, which opened.

Father Hawkshaw was taken aback by the suddenness of it. "Come out then," the priest said. "Come forth and be judged."

Out of the shadow of the mortuary, a bloated foot and cankle appeared and the stained floral print dress Mrs. Novak wore the day she died. The face was discolored, the eyes still bulged, but it was her. Dyed red hair and all. Confusion evident on her face, she shambled out into the light.

"Mrs... Mrs. Novak?" Father Hawkshaw blurted.

The crowd hushed and pulsed away from the seemingly revived woman. From the trees and rooftops, crows watched the display of the dead mingling with the living.

"Well, it sure isn't Greta Garbo, you old fool," Wendy Novak croaked, her jowls shaking as though she sneezed. "Now, kindly get the hell out of my way, I'm missing my stories, and I know Jim let that dumb mutt off the chain." She waddled through the onlookers and grumbled at their gawking faces.

"You ready to believe, padre?" Jesus asked as he came out into the parking lot. "Or is there something else? Honestly, I don't know how much time I've got left, but I'll spend it converting you."

Before the priest could answer, the onlookers rushed Jesus and hoisted him on their shoulders. "Hail the Second Coming! Hail Jesus of Greet Grit!" they said as they threw him higher. All the jostling and grabbing shook Jesus' arm from the socket. The skin gave way and the appendage flopped to the ground. "Someone get a bandage for Jesus!" the crowd shouted. Through the mass of people, a purple cloth gripped by an old hand emerged. It was Father Hawkshaw, stole in hand, tears streaming down his face.

Jesus took the stole with a smile and said, "I'm a forgiver, padre, and this too will be forgiven." The people tied his arm onto the shoulder and fell to their knees in prayer.

Jesus looked at them and smirked.

When Crazy Doris Johnson came to his side, Jesus whispered, "Thank God she wailed on those kids. But, let's get out of here. I could use a drink and there's a couple of crows eyeing me funny."

Jesus started to the Live-Oak with the multitude at his heels, singing his praises.

VIII.

Jesus never got into the Live-Oak. The witnesses to his miracles surrounded him in the parking lot, hoping to hear him speak. They called for something more than just the events of the past week. They wanted something to guide them. Someone to lead them down a path they never knew they neglected to travel. And, leading the chant, Father Hawkshaw cried and looked on Jesus with the eyes of man possessed or a man broken.

Lorenzo Giraldo brought out pitchers of beer for the people and let Jesus sit on the front steps of the Live-Oak.

Despite the stink wafting off his skin, Jesus sat in the sun and drank the cold beer quickly, letting it soak through his shredded skin. His arm still hung off his shoulder, kept close only by the purple stole the priest gave him. After his second beer, Jesus looked out at the people and said, "I'm really not sure what you guys are looking for."

"We want salvation," someone said. "We want to know the way."

"Well, damn," Jesus said. "Don't look at me like I'm some light off in the distance."

"How did you do it?" another shouted. "How did you escape death?"

Jesus rubbed at his face and sighed. "I can't tell you how I got here, but I can tell you how I got *there*. How I lived. Now, I know there aren't a whole lot of you that can think back to me before all this, but there's something to it. I always said to live and let live. The way I see it, yeah, you might look at the next guy and think he's doing something wrong, and maybe he even is, but that doesn't mean shit. I don't need to single anyone out. Every one of you knows it. You look out at someone and think of all the things you don't like, hell, maybe even hate. But, you don't think about what kind of a mess you are. I knew a guy once, used to say that he hated dopers and he said it over his ninth fucking beer."

"Preach it!" Abe von Snowdon blurted.

"But, you've got to be solid about it, people," Jesus went on. "Don't go out spitting bullshit when you don't even believe it. Find out what your rules are and follow them. Hold people to the same standard you hold yourself. Man, I can't tell you how many people—even some that are sitting here--have done some things in this town that I won't even speak of, but when I saw it, I never said a word. You know why? Because I didn't think it was my place, since it wasn't anyone else's place to tell me what they thought about my own goings-on. I wasn't a good man, I'll say it. But, I've never met a good man either. Just a bunch of thieves and liars waiting for their chance to be thieves and liars. If it's Lorenzo here charging two bucks a beer when he only pays fifty cents or when the mayor only cracked down on the working girls that turned him down."

"Amen!" one of the multitude shouted.

"Thank you, sister," Jesus said. "I don't know what to tell you. Just, I don't know… all of you know what you like and how you like it. I just say, don't be too quick to snatch it away from anyone else on account of you not living that way. I mean, Doris told me all the junk you said over my grave and I heard all of you in the Live-Oak. But, what I want to know is if any of you really think you were all that much better than me. I'll say this much, I may have been a real piece of shit, but that was who I was, who I *am*. It's how I was made. How all of you were made. So, when you're looking at someone and thinking about all the ways they're a scumbag, think about how they got there. Man, it's like getting mad at the ocean for blocking your way. Is the problem really the water or the way you're going?"

Jesus drank from his mug of beer and was about to say something else when he noticed the crows in the trees. The way they looked at him, the way they hunched as if in unison, spooked him. He knew finally what they were, why they were there. Jesus threw the empty mug at the tree, missing the branches. The mug shattered against the trunk, but the birds were unmoved. "You get away from me!" he shouted at them. "I'm not going back! Never! You all had your chance! I won't go back! There's nothing to drink--"

As though of a single mind, the birds dropped from their perches and swarmed Jesus. He tried to fight them off, as did Crazy Doris Johnson and Father Hawkshaw. The birds pecked at them, clawed at their faces, and pushed them further away from Jesus. The crowd watched the birds devour Jesus in tiny bites. Though they beat at them with blankets and shirts and hats and whipped at them with belts and rosaries, the crows only danced away and swung around to attack Jesus from another angle. Soon, Jesus was on one knee, then that too was torn from him. The crows cawed and pecked and tore until there was nothing left but the bones and the barbed-wire.

Then, as quickly as they attacked, they scattered into the sky.

The multitude looked at the pile of bones in silence. As one, they were shocked and amazed, unable to move. Then, Father Hawkshaw fell to his knees and crawled over to the bones, picking a bit of finger from the folds of his now ruined stole. He wrapped the finger, the skull, and some other bones in the stole and rose with them. "Come now, my flock," he sobbed. "He may not have been here long, but he has carved the way of the righteous. Let us build a new church, one worthy of Jesus of Green Grit County, and let us serve him well."

—ETC.—

Small Truths

It happened while Jim Pequeño was shaving in the morning. Half his face was still covered in the shaving cream his hot lather dispenser produced. It was a bulky contraption that took up too much room on the sink, but Jim didn't remember it taking up *that* much. As he shaved, the room seemed to get bigger and bigger. At first, his waist was at the countertop, then his chest. His own eyes were confused as the mirror and sink grew and his reflection could not reach the mirror anymore. He wondered why the world grew around him. Even the razor in his hand grew to the size of a war hammer before he had to drop it.

When the room stopped changing, Jim was nude and lost in the jumbled folds of his bath towel. He climbed out of the towel and tried to wipe his face with it, but it was like trying to pull a semi-truck by its door. Jim wiped his face like a penitent man and stood and looked around.

The bathroom was still the same. Cube-ish and tall. The old toilet still had the faint stains of previous owners and Jim's own late night urinations. The flowered plunger-holder stood like a tower and the raised shower seemed a different world he could never hope to reach. "Help!" he yelled. "Help! Monica! Jerry! Suzie! Anyone! Help!"

The sounds of his family starting their day were evident, but it seemed they could not hear him. Jim climbed off the towel hill and started for the bathroom door. The grout of the beige tiles was a wide lane to him with many ruts and grooves. Looking around, the sheer amount of hair on the floor was amazing. The strands were thick as ropes and trying to move one exhausted him. At the door, Jim looked under it and up at it. He reached as high as he could, but, even jumping, he wouldn't be able to move it.

He heard his wife calling for him. "Jim? Where are you?"

"Monica, I'm in here!" he shouted. "I think… I shrunk! I'm only--" he started and looked around to gauge his size. "I'm only a centimeter tall! Please help me!" But, he soon figured his small size distorted everything. It made the sound his vocal chords produced tiny and dead by the time they reached his wife's ankles.

Someone tried the bathroom door. They found it unlocked and swung it open. The air displaced by the door sent Jim tumbling through the room along with melon-sized dust motes and the giant strands of hair. It was his son, Jerry.

The boy, fifteen and pudgy, looked in the room. "He's not in here, ma," Jerry said.

"Well, where could he be?" she asked him from down the hall.

"I don't know," Jerry said. "Did he have a meeting this morning?"

"Maybe," Monica shouted.

"No!" Jim shouted as he crept to the base of the toilet bowl. "I'm down here! Damn it! Hear me! Hear me!"

"Well," Monica said. "I'll call him after lunch. Now, hurry up in there. Your sister needs to get ready for school too."

"I know, I know," Jerry said and went in, locking the door twice before turning on the faucet. He saw Jim's razor on the floor. He lifted it, shrugged, and tossed it onto the rim of the sink. Though the water ran, Jerry did nothing with it. Instead, he went to the toilet and undid his pants. He sat, his bare thighs plopping against the toilet seat like a thunderclap. The squeak of the loose toilet seat was like the roar of a jet engine.

Jim hid beneath the toilet, hoping that, in his current state, smells wouldn't be bigger too.

But, there were no smells. Just sounds. A rhythmic slapping of hand and skin. Jim moved around to see what the sound was. Past the crumpled jeans and bare knees, he saw clearly what his son was doing. One hand stroked while the other held up his cell phone, where pictures and short films of insanely large breasted women rubbing vegetable oil over their dinner-plate nipples flashed. Gagging, Jim returned to the spot behind the toilet. He hoped the boy wouldn't take long.

But, as he sat there, back to the base of the toilet, he noticed a crack in the wall. He went to it and noted some of the wood splintered by time. He thought he could use it to get the attention of someone, anyone, who came into the bathroom. He found a good splinter and tried to tear it free. As it broke, something inside the wall stirred. Splinter held like a short spear, Jim backed away, the drumbeat of his son's masturbation matching the pounding of his heart.

From the dark, a single black ant poked its head out, flapping its antennae wildly. It was the size of a small horse and snapped its mandibles in the air. Jim stood before it, ready. The ant, blind and dumb, felt the floor and came on aimlessly. It meandered on an old dead trail and eventually found Jim. The slap of its antennae felt like a punch on Jim's thigh. "Hey! God damn it!" he shouted, swinging his splinter. If the ant noticed the strike, it didn't show it. It advanced slowly, its mandibles clicking a sound only Jim could hear. Jim stabbed at the black ant, scoring a deep line across its forehead. The ant quickly retreated, turning and moving through pheromone laced switch-backs until it was in the safety of the wall again. "Christ," Jim huffed. "I swear, if I get out of this, I won't bitch about fumigating again."

Jerry was almost finished, if his odd groans were any indication.

"God! Hurry it up, son!" Jim shouted, but he knew only the ants could hear him.

His son kissed his phone as he cleaned himself up.

Jim felt sick. He wondered if it was from the odor of disinfectant or the stale fart smell that hung over everything. But, he thought, it was more likely from being witness to his son stroking a cock the size of a 747's fuselage.

Suzie knocked on the door. "C'mon, Jer. You've been in there for like an hour. I need to get ready already."

"Hold on, hold on," Jerry spat. "I was just finishing up." His son pulled up his pants and washed his hands under the running water. As if an after-thought, Jerry flushed the toilet, washing away the evidence.

His children crossed paths in the doorway, exchanging snide looks. "She's all yours, sis," Jerry said.

The door closed. Jim ran behind the toilet again.

Suzie did the same as her brother: turned on the faucet, undid her pants, and sat on the toilet. The sound of a thin box being torn open and the thick contents sliding out resounded in the room like an avalanche, but, still, Jim wouldn't look, holding his splinter like a Roman sentry. "Easy to use application strip," he heard Suzie say as she tossed the empty box to the ground. He strafed the toilet to look at it.

On the box, a woman in her thirties smiled as if relieved and the words, "Price Mart Economy Pregnancy Test" were written on it in a soothing blue. "What!" he screamed, but by the way his daughter, his sweet little sixteen year old girl, continued to examine the plastic test, he knew she couldn't hear him.

"Urinate on the absorbent strip and wait one hundred and twenty seconds... sad face indicates pregnancy and the happy face indicates non-pregnancy. Ninety five percent accurate. See money saving coupon in box for one dollar off an additional test." She stuck the test into the toilet bowl and started. She cursed when the pee stream splashed on her hand.

Jim didn't even think she knew curses like that.

Then, they waited. The father below the shadow of a porcelain monolith and the daughter atop it, legs splayed out before her.

Jim counted the time by heartbeats. One minute. Two minutes.

Suzie lifted the test to the light to examine it. "Oh, thank you fucking God!" she sighed. Immediately, she wrapped the test in toilet paper and put it back in the box. From her crumpled jeans, Suzie took out a cell phone and dialed. Even the dull ring was louder. Like the grumblings of a whale's belly. "Hey, Carl. Yeah, I just took it and... we're in the clear." A shout of jubilation came from the other end. "I know. I guess my stupid dad won't be forcing me to be the next Mrs. Carl LaManti anytime soon. But, I swear Carl, you better pull out next time, I mean it. You too. Bye."

"Carl LaManti!" Jim fumed. "That... that... burnout!" He ranted and raved, swinging his splinter up at her. "How could you! You're only sixteen! I raised you right!" he yelled as she walked out of the bathroom.

All through the house, the sound of feet shuffling on the carpet and doors slamming vibrated so much that Jim thought them earthquakes. Soon, the house was silent except for a distant murmur of a television. "Monica!" he yelled, hoping that maybe one of them by some miracle could hear him. "Monica, come in here! You've got to help me. We need to save the kids! Help!"

No one came. The only thing to stir was an ant from the crack in the wall. "Great!" Jim called out and ran to it like a savage. He beat at its legs, snapping one off and breaking another. Jim kept calling it Carl as he fought it back to its hole. "Fuck you, Carl! Fuck you, you fucking piece of fucking shit!" he ranted, striking it like a lunatic. The injured ant retreated, leaving Jim alone with his tiny spear and his thoughts. He sat with his back to the toilet base, wishing he'd just finished shaving and gone to work. He wasn't sure of how or why this had suddenly happened to him, but he knew his boss wouldn't care what his excuses were. Mr. Gustavo Menchaca was a demanding and often abusive boss, but at least afterward Jim could come back home to his normal son and loving daughter, not the sex-fiend and the whore.

For hours, he tried to shake what he'd seen from his memory.

A lack of breakfast caused his stomach to rumble. He tried to will it away, but it persisted. Jim thought of venturing out to the kitchen but knew the walk would take an eternity. And, even if he made it, there was nothing he could do save find a forgotten crumb and gorge on that. Suddenly, he looked at the broken ant leg sitting a few steps away.

Once, as a child, Jim had accidentally eaten ants that had found their way into his morning cereal. When he panicked, his father told him, "Don't worry, son. It's just protein." With that in mind, he went up to the leg and examined it. Bent and sectioned, it hardly seemed appetizing. His stomach growled.

The first bite broke one of his teeth.

Jim howled and spat the broken tooth. Apparently, the armored shells of ants were effective to a creature of Jim's size. He tried to suck the meat from the gory end, but it tasted foul and rank, He threw the leg at the hole in the wall, and, after a time, an ant came to collect it. "Take it you sons of bitches," he cried, massaging his jaw.

The sound of bare feet shook the ground and Monica opened the bathroom door.

What now, he thought.

Monica had her cell phone in her hand and dialed frantically. "Hi," she said. "It's me… No, I don't know where Jim is… I thought he left to work early… What do you mean he didn't show up? That's not like him."

A gruff voice said something to her. Monica laughed.

"Oh, I doubt it," she giggled. "I don't think Jim has it in him to cheat on me. Oh, don't you start. You always do that. I don't think I could ever… you know, leave him. He's so good to me and the kids. I mean, he's not even here and I'm still hiding in the bathroom, talking to you. All this sneaking around is just… exciting. I know it'll kill him, but… I can't help it."

The voice replied.

"Oh, stop it, Gus," Monica chided. "I'm not jumping into the shower. No, no. But, let's see if we can't squeeze one in later. The Flamingo Inn? That sounds good. Last time, they had such great champagne, even if we did have to drink it out of plastic cups."

"Gus?" Jim said, his face twisting. "Gus? Gus… tavo! Gustavo Menchaca! You filthy bitch! How could you! With that fat slob!" He took the splinter in both hands and ran like a pole-vaulter. "You bitch! I'll kill you!" he shouted.

It seemed to take forever to get to her, but once Jim did, he put all of his weight behind the stab to the side of her foot.

"Yeow!" she gasped, jerking her foot back in pain.

Jim couldn't move in time. Her foot engulfed him in shadow before shattering everything below his ribs. His ruined body stuck to her foot like gum and as Monica talked to Gustavo, she flicked Jim off behind the toilet The last things he heard were the sounds of his wife giggling.

Later, once Jerry was home from school, he ran to the bathroom and masturbated to big-boob fetish videos he'd downloaded, not wondering what four sugar ants ate in the corner of the bathroom. When he was done, he used the toilet paper he cleaned himself with to smash them all and toss the corpses--human and ant--into the waiting toilet.

—ETC.—

The Wrong Side of the Mule

I.

The bandits struck Fort Palmer at night. Forty strong, the mix of exiled Apaches and Mexican thieves shot two rangers on the wall before the great wooden doors were shut and bolted. The rangers there numbered just over sixteen, now that the watchmen were mortally wounded and groaned in the dirt as the bullets cooled in their chests. With the high fort walls and provisions, the troop would've cut the bandit's numbers, but the moonless night had them firing with nothing but rifles flashes to guide their shots throughout the surrounding area. The bandits, however, had the benefit of the rangers' watch fires and oil lamps and the long shadows they cast. Luckily, the Franklin Peaks to the north made encircling the fort impossible for all but the most skilled riders.

The rangers held Fort Palmer for three days, not daring to step foot outside the walls lest they be shot and skinned by some hidden Apache. But, the longer they waited, so too did their assailants. Every night, the rangers saw distant fires where the bandits no doubt cooked game snared or shot. The bandits kept a constant volley of fire, an almost endless series of reports and pops against the thick walls of Fort Palmer as though all the lead in Mexico came against them now.

By the sixth day, the rangers had decided to butcher one of the old mares.

With supplies dwindling, Captain Hinton ordered three of the men to take a written decree demanding food and munitions from the town of Franklin, which sat a three-day's ride away on the other side of the peaks. "The good people of Texas'll give all they can! Just you see!" Captain Hinton shouted before promoting McAlpin, a scrawny man of forty, to lieutenant and the other two--Fitzsimmons and Barclay--to full rangers. With the promise of more pay and a few slices of the butchered horse, the trio made for the mountains behind them by night as the remaining rangers tried to fire with a bit more abandon in hopes of distracting the bandits.

II.

In Franklin, the general store was owned by an old Mexican named Gabriel, a man known for his hatred of Captain Hinton since the day the old ranger shot him in the foot for hassling him over an outstanding bill. When McAlpin entered the store, Gabriel limped over from behind the counter and nodded to them wordlessly. Fitzsimmons and Barclay began combing the store for the items they needed. But, both men stopped their search through the dusty aisles when McAlpin started to shout.

"What the hell do you mean!" he cried, his slim voice visibly irritating Gabriel. "That's an official document by Captain Nicholas Hinton and sanctioned by the authority of the state of Texas."

The old Mexican looked at the document and smirked. "This paper would've been worth more if your captain hadn't scribbled all over it," he told McAlpin, handing it back. "I know how this all works. I give you cartridges and food and horses, and I'll never get paid. Your captain would hang me when I ask for the money."

"Fort Palmer is under attack as we speak!" McAlpin went on. "Men are dying while you're worried about money! Half of those men have families!"

"What of my family, gringo? Huh? Most I'll give you is two bags of beans, a sack of corn, three mules, and three boxes of shells," Gabriel said while he looked McAlpin over. "And that's for all your rifles and that one's sidearm," he said, motioning to Barclay, who wore his father's Colt .45 with a rosewood grip.

"Leave two guns for our caravan and we'll die," McAlpin told him. "We'd be defenseless if some Apache came gunning for us. Hell, even a couple of wolves--"

Gabriel snorted and limped further down the long counter. From beneath it, he pulled out a dirty machete and slid it to the ranger. "There," he said. "A fighting chance. More than you tejanos have ever given me or mine. Now, do we have a deal?"

After a long time, McAlpin grumbled, "Let me see the mules." Barclay was vocal about having to give away a family treasure that survived Apache raids and Comanche hunts for a mangy set of mules and food not fit for convicts, but McAlpin, pulling rank, told him it was his duty to the rangers, to Texas.

"The hell do you know?" Barclay snapped. "Only reason you got any rank is 'cause you were the closest to the captain when he was handing them out. Longest career as a private in company history, ain't that right, lieutenant?"

"Boy, I'll sell your scrawny ass if it means getting another box of shells, so you just watch it," McAlpin shot back. "Now, give the man your pistol. Maybe those bandits'll have a better one on them."

"He's just asking for all our stuff on account of the captain, the son of a bitch," Barclay said. He emptied his pistol of bullets and pocketed them before handing it to Gabriel.

"Is it true you paid a witch to curse him?" Fitzsimmons asked as he turned over his rifle.

Gabriel took the gun, unbreached the round, and handed it to the young ranger. "You know Hinton, right?"

"Sure," the ranger said. "Been at Fort Palmer a year, now."

"Then you'd know the man doesn't need the devil's help being cursed," Gabriel chuckled. "A man so stupid he'd drown in the desert." Once the rifles were collected, Gabriel told them to take the food and bullets out to the back of the store where the mules were kept.

The mules were a sorry bunch that seemed merely the skins of pack animals stretched over and held there by matted fur and flies. Two were mud-colored while the third was almost jet black with drooped eyelids. When the first of the packs were put upon them, the rangers thought the animals would tremble and collapse, but, with a snort, the beasts of burden held the supplies. Each of the men took a mule: McAlpin took the most agreeable of the brown mules, leaving the other to Fitzsimmons. Barclay took the black one by the lead rope and began to follow the others, but the rope snapped taut.

The mule strained against the rope as if it knew where the rangers were leading it.

Barclay pulled and spat at the mule, all to no avail. "All right, you four-legged stack of shit," Barclay growled. He went behind the mule and kicked at its flank. When it didn't move, Barclay took the mule by one of its floppy ears and pulled, succeeding in forcing the animal to stretch its neck out further. "I didn't give that old Mex my daddy's gun just to fight with a bag of fleas," Barclay said as he took out his small pocket knife. He showed it to the mule, dangling it in front of the animal's lazy lids. "Now, you going to move? Or am I going to have to get mean?" he asked as he pricked the animal's skin.

The black mule swished its tail and looked at Barclay as if considering the man. Then, it stepped forward.

III.

It was the black mule that held the trio up, making them camp only a few miles from Franklin and still two days of hard travel from reaching Fort Palmer. The mule bit at its rope and snorted and kicked when made to go more than a few feet. It even tossed the bags of food off its back more than once like a child tired of church clothes.

Barclay voted to shoot the animal, but McAlpin assured the ranger that if he killed the mule, Barclay'd be the one to carry the load.

They camped a ways off the path that led into the Franklin Peaks, veering west and wrapping around the lower of the mountain passes. McAlpin ordered Barclay to take the first watch and armed him with the rusty machete and sent him to walk the perimeter. While the young ranger hobbled in the dark, waving the machete in front of him like a blind man, McAlpin dipped into one of the bags of beans and split most of the food with Fitzsimmons.

After three hours, no one came to relieve Barclay of his wandering post. He used the glow of the fire to get back to the camp, stumbling over ropelike roots and catching his pants on thorny brush. When he returned to the camp,

Barclay found the other rangers asleep, his portion of beans burnt black in the pot which hung over the low fire. Barclay moved to kick some of the ashes at the others but stopped when he chanced a look at the mules tied to a nearby tree.

The two brown mules dozed side by side, but the other, the black mule, stood with its eyes open, staring across the fire at Barclay. It may have been a trick of the fire or some other explainable phenomenon that made the mule's eyes glow red for a moment, yet it sent Barclay back a step all the same. As he moved away from the fire, Barclay swore a shadow came from the brush beyond the penumbra of light of their small fire. It was a thing shaped as a man, but embraced by some deformity, some inhuman quality to it. The shadow stretched out an arm of ink to pet the mule's bristly mane.

If it was indeed a trick of the flames or of his weary mind, Barclay couldn't tell, for the shadow was like a half-remembered nightmare. Horribly defined only for an instant.

IV.

A storm fast approaching from the east kicked up the winds, sending grit and dead bushels across the mountain face. It claimed the fire, though Barclay, still fixated on the deformed specter beside the mule, had fed the light kindling all night. The branches above their camp swayed like the trunks of wild elephants, reaching low enough to brush McAlpin's bedroll with its leaves. Once the camp was awake, the lieutenant ordered Barclay and Fitzsimmons to break camp and pack the mules. Barclay complied, keeping silent about what he'd seen. He knew no one would believe him and that any question about his wits would have him doing the worst jobs once they returned to the fort.

The mules were skittish in the wind. They bit at the rangers and bucked the packs from their shoulders, snorting loudly as they did. The black mule, though, kept its eyes on Barclay, occasionally swishing its tail though only a few flies were on it.

With McAlpin's mule packed and Fitzsimmons struggling with the other, Barclay moved to pack the food and bedrolls on the black mule, which put up no resistance despite the torrential sound of the wind cutting through the trees. As Barclay tightened the foodstuff to the mule's back, the wind grew more violent, swaying the trees spastically.

The branch tearing off the tree made a horrifying sound and crashed onto the party. McAlpin, who'd chased his map to a nearby bush, watched Barclay and Fitzsimmons disappear beneath the dismembered hand of the tree. One second seeing them with their shocked faces pointed to the branches and in the next, there was only foliage. Barclay and the black mule were only whipped and scraped by the thin twigs. But, Fitzsimmon's mule made gurgling pleas from beneath the leaves.

The branch all but impaled Fitzsimmons, who, once uncovered, was open for the rangers to see. The shredded branch claimed a chunk from the man's chest and nearly tore his arm from his shoulder. The mule, its back broken, was pinned under the heavy branch and struggled pathetically, extending its neck and kicking its forelegs while the hind legs lay twisted and lifeless in a growing puddle of Fitzsimmon's blood. Beneath the jumble of twisted limbs was Fitzsimmon's pistol, warped and crusted with dirt.

Barclay stood over the gore, turned, and vomited.

McAlpin went over to the shivering ranger who prayed up to the sky in a dying's gibberish, muttered a few words of his own, and shot him in the head. Next, he went to the mule and put it out of its misery.

"Load up the packs on the ones that made it," McAlpin said, gripping his coat against the wind. "The fort's under attack and our men need these supplies." When Barclay didn't immediately move, he spat, "That's an order from your superior, Ranger."

"How can you not bury him? Coyotes will scatter him all over Texas," Barclay said. He was still pale from the sight of the damaged creatures. "Spent a year with the man and that doesn't deserve a proper burial?"

"We'll bury what's left of him after we get to Fort Palmer," McAlpin said, turning away from the twitching mule. "The fort's under attack, and take it from me, if those bandits get through… It'll make Fitz's fate look like just rewards. They'll skin the fort to a man, wear them like trophies on their other raids. The ones that don't die outright… those savages'll take turns with 'em. Raping 'em and stabbing out their eyes… boiling their brains with hot pokers…"

"But Fitz--"

"Fitz signed his ass over to the rangers," McAlpin said. "Texas comes first. Rangers second. You, last. Now, split the packs between the two mules. That's an order," McAlpin spat then went to his maps as best as the wind allowed.

After a moment, Barclay moved over to the fallen mule and set to untying the blood-stained packs. All the while, the black mule watched and swished its tail.

V.

Despite the wind, the trail they used should've brought them over the peaks and into view of the fort in the distance. But, the black mule resisted the march at every turn no matter how many times Barclay whipped or kicked it. Only with the prodding of his folding knife did the young ranger manage to move the disagreeable pack animal.

The storm responsible for the wind moved in quickly. The clouds were thick, almost blackening the sky, and lit up with tendrils of lightning. Yet, while both men expected a heavy rain, only a drizzle covered the mountainside. The constant mist stuck their shirts and pants to their skin, making each step awkward and weighty. The switchbacks were soaked down to the stone and each step was an exercise in agility. Barclay found himself slipping the steeper the winding path went, each time coming up off the ground covered in yellow mud. No matter how much he tried to wipe it away, all he did was spread it around. The drizzle did little to wash the mud from Barclay's body, giving him the appearance of a cancerous golem.

The worst of it was the packs of food. The longer it drizzled around them, the quicker their food would turn to mush. And, from the look of the clouds above them, the wet misery would last for the day at least.

McAlpin outdistanced Barclay by over thirty yards. His mule, it seemed to Barclay, was as interested in getting off the mountain as the rangers were. It kept pace with the lieutenant, shaking its head only to dry itself somewhat and move on.

The black mule, though, was as solid as an anchor. Barclay found himself tugging the lead rope with every step only to have the mule relinquish an inch or two. The young ranger took to cursing at the animal, shouting so long the mud stuck on his cheeks leaked into his mouth, which only made the ranger shout louder as he chewed on the grit.

It was during a colorful rant about the mule and a Comanche slave trader that McAlpin stopped and tied his mule to a shrub. He made his way to Barclay, who didn't even notice his commanding officer's approach, too engrossed in pulling wildly and slipping into the mud. "Boy, would you shut the hell up already," McAlpin spat. "There's bandits all over the other side of that peak and it stands to reason they might send a few over here to block supplies. Keep hollering and carrying on and you're liable to get us shot."

Barclay stood as a figure of mud and huffed each breath. "How're we going to fight any damn bandits with your pistol and a machete not fit to cut paper?" He snorted and pulled at the mule.

McAlpin narrowed his eyes and spat. "Boy, I'm getting tired of that lip. Just lead the damn mule. Keep up this chickenshit pace and the fort'll be nothing but a bone yard when we get there. Don't worry, though, kid. I'll tell all their widows they've got to grieve on account of you not being able to pull a pea-brained lummox."

"Ain't no lummox," Barclay said. "This here piece of shit'll be the death of us. What we've got here is a little slice of hell on four legs. Touched by the devil, this one is."

"Enough with that," McAlpin said. "You're sounding worse than a preacher at a revival. Now, keep your trap shut. That mule's a mule like any other," the lieutenant said as the drizzle picked up. "I expect you to pace me else I'll make *you* carry the saddlebags," McAlpin said as he turned to go up the trail, but the rain rolled down the mountainside in torrents, forcing him to strafe the rocky terrain. Ahead, the mule pawed at the ground as muddy streams drained around it. "I'm too old and tired to protect Texas all on my lonesome. Why I--"

Then, a chunk of the peaks broke.

The stone fell, taking boulder sized pieces down with it. To McAlpin and Barclay, it looked as though it were all a mirage. One minute, a mule nervously pawed at a path. In the next, there was a wall of broken stone and a single hoof sitting in a pool of blood mixing with slate mud that was quickly washed down the mountainside. They stood looking at it, the rain dripping off their soaked clothes. The black mule swished its tail.

McAlpin rubbed his forehead and looked behind them. "Let me go up that way and see if we can't go around this mudslide," he said. "And get that mule up to that boulder over there. No damn excuses neither! If the fort's doomed, it sure won't be on my account," he told the ranger as he passed.

Barclay watched the lieutenant backtrack and attempt to find some way up. Once McAlpin was out of sight, Barclay tried to turn the mule around, but it wouldn't move. He pushed its neck, kicked at it, and punched at the creature, but Barclay couldn't do more than make it turn its head.

The young ranger tried pulling with the rope once more but fell when his boot heel slid on a loose patch of earth. Barclay got to his knees and growled. He looked at the mule in the face, snarling, "All right, you mongrel, what the hell do I have to do to get you to move?" At first, he stared down the mule as an act of animalistic intimidation in hopes of scaring it. But, the longer he looked at the lazy stare, the more lost in the rich blackness of them Barclay became. In those eyes, Barclay saw something unknowable and deep in the memories of his very cells, something infinite and horrible just beyond sight, just beyond memory. In those eyes, he saw the world as the illusion it truly was through the geometric trails of celestial veins within the mule's black eyes.

Barclay chuckled. "I sure can," he laughed at the mule. "I'll give him to you. Never could stand the son of a bitch."

The mule looked at Barclay, who swore there was a glint of red in them.

Then, with a snort, the mule turned around.

VI.

All the next morning, Barclay thought of killing McAlpin. He formulated plans on those slippery mountain trails. At first, he thought of just stealing the man's gun and shooting him dead, but dismissed the idea. Too many variables were involved, too many chances for things to go wrong. The pistol could jam or he could slip and bounce down the mountain. Barclay would also have to get close enough to snatch the pistol. McAlpin was not a large man, but had an iron jaw and wiry muscle. On more than one occasion, Barclay himself found those facts out after nights of heavy drinking in the fort.

The idea of pushing McAlpin off the sheer ledges they used crossed the young ranger's mind, but that too was dismissed. The more he visualized it, the more Barclay scoffed at the idea. McAlpin might, with Barclay's luck, only fall and break his leg, leaving Barclay with the task of collecting him or pulling the mule to him. That was, of course, if McAlpin didn't grab hold of him and take him along on the drop.

As night drew upon them, Barclay settled on a plan. He'd stab McAlpin as he slept. Barclay knew he'd get the first watch, as he always did. All he had to do then was wait until McAlpin fell asleep. The drip of rain would mask any sound Barclay'd make. There was the chance McAlpin would awaken and fight back, but any doubt the young ranger had fled once he looked into the dark mule's eyes. In those black orbs, he felt comfort and confidence in a plan and even took his pocketknife from the holster on his belt.

Barclay held it in his closed fist until they made camp under a craggy shelf that shielded them from most of the annoying rain. They found enough dried roots and grasses to start a small fire, which they used to dry their clothes. The flame wasn't strong and wouldn't last long, so the two men didn't bother cooking. Instead, they took a pinch of raw corn softened by the rain and chewed it. McAlpin took out his map, which lay in almost translucent strips before the fire.

"Tomorrow," the lieutenant breathed. "We'll head up the western path until it forks. Then, it's the same trail we used to get out of the fort. We'll make it by evening if this pace keeps up and the weather breaks, god willing."

Barclay stared at him from across the fire, the folding knife still in his hand. "How long have they been pinned down?" he asked. "A week? That's a long time to eat horse and spend ammo. Do you think there'll even be a fort when we get off this pile of rocks?"

McAlpin glared at the ranger and spat. "Damn, kid. Few days of an ornery mule and you're thinking we're out doing this for our health. Fort Palmer's there, standing proud. If they save their shots, our boys can shoot for a month, and those old nags might be tough as boot leather, but they'll keep the boys alive for two solid weeks."

"Yeah," Barclay said after a moment. "Guess you're right."

"I haven't been lieutenant long, but I can tell you, kid, there's a lot for you to learn out here," McAlpin said as he placed stones on the strips of map to keep them from possibly blowing away. He then found a spot deep beneath the crag to sleep once he cleared it of whip-spiders and other multi-legged denizens of the mount. "Wake me up in a few hours," he told Barclay. "You'll get the first watch tonight."

"Figured I would," Barclay said. He turned to the rain so that McAlpin couldn't see his grin. He glanced at the mule beyond the fire, whose shadow bounced long and spider-like on the rocky wall. Beside the shadow, another figure's shape formed beside the mule, but no matter how much Barclay focused on the air around the mule, he couldn't discern anything there.

Barclay waited out an hour staring at the storm, watching the water cling to the crag before being lost in the endless gray. Once Barclay felt the time was right, he removed his boots and peeled off his rancid socks. He spread them by the embers of the dying fire and eyed McAlpin as he crouched. Barclay opened his knife slowly, careful not to let the lock click too loudly. With eyes ever on McAlpin, the young ranger crept over to the man, knife poised to strike. As he made his slow way to the man, Barclay decided that stabbing at McAlpin's neck would be best. But, when he was close enough to finish him, McAlpin turned over, giving Barclay his back.

The young ranger stopped and chanced a glance at the black mule. Its eyes glowed almost imperceptibly. Then, it seemed to gesture approval, though it could've been simply trying to get dry.

Barclay nodded to the animal and got his balance. With one hand, he pinned down McAlpin's head and stabbed him with the other. The lieutenant struggled. He kicked. He gurgled. Still Barclay stabbed him repeatedly, chipping ribs and puncturing the man's organs until McAlpin's torso held only a soup of viscera and blood. The young ranger held the man down until the blood drained from him and most of the fight had fled. "Come on, then," Barclay told the mule.

The creature didn't move.

The creature didn't move.

"Oh, I get it," Barclay said and scoffed. "A deal was a deal." The young ranger took hold of McAlpin's ankles, though they weakly tried to kick free, and dragged him over to the mule, where he dropped the man's feet roughly. "He's all yours," Barclay chuckled as he sat down to watch the mule. The creature sniffed at the dying man, nudged him with its long snout, then bit him on the forehead. When McAlpin yelped, the mule stared at Barclay for a moment before chomping over McAlpin's ashen face, seemingly breathing in the man's weak screams.

VII.

It took a night of chewing in the dark, but by morning the mule had eaten McAlpin down to his ankles, leaving only unrecognizable gristle and tattered clothes behind for the mountain birds. Barclay himself couldn't stand the sound of it. The square teeth squeaking on pulverized bones, flesh tearing like wet clothes. But, with McAlpin dead and the mule complacent, Barclay could finally get to the fort and be off that mountain. The supplies, mostly mold and mush, would be needed until any further aid came their way.

Barclay imagined his return to Fort Palmer and went through his explanation over and over again. Fitzsimmons had been killed by a falling branch and no more needed to be said. McAlpin, however, would be another story. At first, Barclay thought to say bandits had ambushed them too. But, with only a knife and one pistol, Captain Hinton would ask how Barclay survived to bring them one mule loaded with supplies. Then, the thought of the mudslide came to mind. That would explain Barclay's survival and the missing McAlpin. By the time anyone got around to looking for the lieutenant, there'd be no body to be found, though Barclay'd blame coyotes or bandits and not the black mule.

Confident in his plan, Barclay kicked the remainder of McAlpin's body off the high path into a thicket of spindly shrubs. Even if they didn't believe his story about the rest, there'd be no proof that he was lying, that he was somehow responsible for any of it.

The mule followed him obediently.

The rains had died during the night and were replaced by a dense fog. From a few feet away, Barclay couldn't see protruding boulders until nearly bumping into the hulking shapes. Worse still, the outline of the path was hazy and the distance of drops masked. If he kicked a pebble off the trail, it simply disappeared without a sound as though never existing. Barclay's only way to go forward was by always moving uphill.

As the trail turned and descended, the summit of Mt. Franklin looming above them, Barclay stopped and tried to discern which path to use, but the rains had washed rocks and mud over any trail they may have used before. He patted himself down for the map but realized he'd thrown it into the dwindling fire to dry his socks.

After a while, Barclay chose a thin trail mostly free of damage and led the mule to it. The mule kept up with him, never hesitating in its steps, pressing ever forward though Barclay found himself nearly strafing the walls.

The fog was thick around them when Barclay heard stones clattering up ahead. He stopped to listen, but as he felt the noise would repeat, a shadow moved in his peripheral vision. Barclay tried to follow the amorphous shape, but when he looked, it was gone. The mule stood behind him, swishing its tail, and waited for Barclay to move again.

All through the day, blanketed by an opaque nothing, Barclay was assailed with thoughts of shadows like the one he saw nights before. Their outline alone frightened him, and he'd once seen Chief Buffalo Horn take a freshly removed head and tie it to his spear, eyes still blinking dumbly. What more, the sounds of approach bounced around the rocky terrain, even beside him where he knew there to be a long drop. With each step, Barclay's nerve was whittled down to a thin cord of sanity. He went from one confident stride after another to a shaky step every few minutes, fearful of the shadows hovering out of sight like bats.

And, with every fearful glance he threw behind him, the mule was there to greet him with its bored expression.

With each passing minute on the cliffside, the world felt smaller. The width of the trail narrowed until Barclay's toes hung over the edge. He was too frightened to look anywhere but forward. But, with each step, he felt the mule keeping up with him. For each one of his nervous steps, the mule walked confidently as though it were traversing a wide city lane. The fog thickened and the shadows fluttered so near, Barclay felt their wings on his cheeks. It got to be that Barclay didn't know what to fear more, staying on the cliff or falling off it.

Finally, Barclay started screaming at the empty air, pleading with it in gibberish.

It was then that the mule nudged the terrified man.

When their eyes locked, Barclay's terror ceased. In those eyes, the young ranger found an alien logic, a philosophy that led to his easy breathing, his distraction from the shadows milling in the air. The key to freedom from the mountain, the key to reaching the fort in time, lay in the ideas flooding Barclay's mind. All he had to do, the mule showed him, was offer himself to it. Give himself up to the beast.

Facing the sheer weight of the gray, Barclay nodded and stuttered his agreement, before taking the folding knife from his pocket and slicing open his palm. He held out his cupped palm for the mule to drink. "Please… help me!" Barclay cried.

The mule sniffed the warm offering and drank. When the black mule had licked the wound clean, it swished its tail and remained still.

At first, Barclay thought the offering was rejected. Yet, once he looked around him, he noticed the fog thinning, the landscape materializing. More and more, the path they stood on became less and less menacing in the light of day. Barclay looked through the thinning fog and there seemed a spot in the distance that shined and danced like a lake in the morning light. He wondered what it could be since there were no lakes near Fort Palmer.

Once the fog fully receded, the beacon was easy to discern.

Fort Palmer was burning. The blaze engulfed the whole of the building and walls and extended to the dry brush around it. All along the road the bandits used, makeshift crosses had been set. On them, the bodies of tortured rangers were masses of frantic buzzards, all pecking and gouging at the tender flesh. They'd all been tortured before being nailed to saltires made from beams taken from the fort.

Barclay couldn't speak as the walls fell and crashed, belching black smoke and star-like embers. The ranger turned to the mule and found it was not alone. Beside the mule, the deformed shadow, rendered wretched in its tangibility, reached a twisted claw out for him to take.

VIII.

A day before news of the fallen fort filtered into town, Gabriel was busy stocking his shelves with new product. The pistols he'd taken from the rangers were expensive and, even sold at a considerable discount, he made a hefty profit from them. He used it, that first night, to get drunk and spend the night with one of the town's dusty prostitutes. The rest went to the store. It was in the middle of his stocking that he heard the fence outside crack and fall.

He limped outside, a pistol in his hand, but he didn't find any thieves or kids messing around his property. Instead, he found the pens where he kept his animals open, the door torn off its hinges. Inside the pens, the mules and donkey's snorted and whinnied. When he rounded the corner to have all the pens in front of him, he noted the addition of a mule he sold days before.

The black mule, covered in mud flecked with gore, munched silently at a trough, straw sticking out of its mouth like broken teeth. Gabriel smiled at it and put his pistol away. "Glad to see you made it back, you mangy piece of shit," he told it and turned back to the storefront. "That'll teach them to watch where they point their fucking guns," he said to no one as he returned to the shade of the store.

—ETC.—

What's with that Roadrunner Down by the Bus Station?

C alles de Lodo, Texas had always been a small town whose biggest population boom in the past decade had been Mrs. Avery's triplets, almost four years ago. Deaths were equally uncommon though inevitable. Dr. A. R. Marx knew this and made a living as the town's physician and mortician, though his work was primarily filled with reading non-fiction books about plane crash survivors and listening to a small TV propped up in the corner of his waiting room, his feet, stuffed into pointed boots, resting on the small coffee table. The years of sitting in the wooden chairs had hunched the doctor into a perpetual stoop.

It was in the middle of a book entitled *Blind Descent* that Dr. Marx received the call from Nico, one of the county paramedics, telling him there'd been an emergency on the outskirts of town. "Well, do you want me to start guessing?" the doctor asked as though he was scolding the receiver. He folded the corner of a page.

"Hispanic male with lacerations to the throat," the paramedic told him. "He's got a weak pulse. Matheson's working on him now, but it doesn't look good. Guy's neck looks like a half-eaten cherry pie."

"That's your professional opinion, I'm guessing," Dr. Marx said as he stretched, his spine cracking loudly. "And, what's with the tongue-and-cheek routine. Spit it out. Who is it?"

"Nestor Piña," Nico said with a chuckle.

"What the hell's funny about that," Dr. Marx snorted. "A man's out there bleeding to death--"

What's with that Roadrunner Down by the Bus Station?

"The old brujo's wife is meeting us at your place," Nico said.

"Aww hell!" Dr. Marx spat. "Did you even try stopping her?"

"Nope," Nico snorted. It was common knowledge that she was scarier than her husband, who they say danced with the devil.

"Thanks for the warning," Dr. Marx said, sarcasm heavy in his voice, and hung up the phone. For a panicked moment, he bounced from one foot to the other, unsure of which direction to go or what medical step to perform next. Olga Piña had that effect on most she met.

A toad-faced woman shaped like a boulder standing alone in the desert, Olga was indeed a hellish woman. The few times Dr. Marx had dealt with her, the woman had been exacting some cruelty on a living thing. She berated the cashiers at Rossman's General until they lowered her total, she threw stones at cats with pinpoint accuracy, and Olga had once gotten out of a Public Intoxication ticket by beating Sheriff Tate with her dusty sandal. Most of the citizens of Calles de Lodo joked that to save his soul from being crushed outright by the sheer intensity of her being, Nestor Piña gave himself up to the safer alternative: the great deceiver. Even Nestor's hellish powers and a bottle of mescal a day were only enough to hold the tidal wave of Olga at bay.

Now, she was on her way to Dr. Marx's office with her husband bleeding to death in a rickety ambulance.

The doctor had barely laid out his sterile materials on the side table in his operating room when he heard the ambulance crunch up the gravel parking lot. It took him a moment to realize the sirens weren't blaring and sighed in relief. Lights and no siren, Marx knew, meant the ambulance carried either a patient suffering from something minor like painful gas or a dead body. From the description Nico gave, Nestor Piña was definitely the latter. Marx's hopes were validated when Nico and Matheson wheeled in the gurney, Nestor Piña laying atop it. The man's neck had been torn open by some type of serrated blade, but Dr. Marx would examine the body once they wheeled him into the operating room, which was also the autopsy lab.

But, any relief Dr. Marx felt with the knowledge that there was no way the death could be blamed on him, quickly disappeared, spooked by the appearance of Olga Piña.

Though a short woman, her presence seemed to occupy the entire waiting room once she came through the door. Her frog face was pressed down into a scowl made cartoonish by the size of her jowls. "Where is my husband?" Olga croaked. "I will see him now." Without waiting for an answer, Olga stomped toward the back of the office to the corridor that led to the various rooms of the clinic/mortuary.

Dr. Marx hesitated a moment before blocking her path. "I-I'm sorry, Mrs. Piña," he said. "I need to examine your husband. I-I'll let you know the moment you can see him."

Olga Piña stopped and narrowed her dark eyes at him. Her throat swelled slightly and she said, "Fine. I'll wait. But be quick. I want all the paperwork dealt with so I can be done with this."

"Of course, of course," Dr. Marx said as he backed into the corridor, not daring to turn his back on the woman as though she were some predator. Cross-armed, Olga watched him like a sentinel.

The corridor had never felt longer, the door handles more elusive, than under the watch of those bloated eyes. Even when Dr. Marx managed to find the room where the paramedics had left Nestor Piña, the weight of that stare followed him. The look of Nestor's wounds, a garish patchwork of intersecting slashes, was dwarfed to the point of triviality against the aura of Olga Piña outside. Before he managed to jot a note about the state of the corpse, Dr. Marx looked at the door repeatedly, expecting Olga to be brooding there.

Even in the cold room, sweat formed on his brow. Dr. Marx wiped at it quickly and put on his surgical mask. He examined the wounds before getting the necessary paperwork, hoping to draft up his report in his head. From the crossing pattern, there had been three cuts, one moving right to left in an upward motion and the other two from left to right forming a messy X. Nestor's skin, usually a rough brown, now seemed the color the old photographs, the gray of unsavory meat. Yet, there was something about Nestor Piña's corpse that didn't seem right. Something that seemed to taunt Dr. Marx without fully coming to light.

Dr. Marx shook the thoughts away, blaming them on nerves and the appearance of Mrs. Piña. There wasn't a soul in Calles de Lodo that claimed to ever have a good experience with Olga Piña, and Dr. Marx didn't think his would be any different. He went to the small filing cabinet that sat beside the wall slots housing Mr. Thomas Holland, an eighty year old man who'd died a week before while watching a televised Formula 1 race and wasn't found until yesterday. Dr. Marx fumbled through the files and found the assessment form. When he turned, he yelped.

Olga Piña stood in the doorway, thick lips scrunched. "What can you tell me?" she asked, though when she said it, it sounded like a threat.

"M… Mrs. Piña," he said after gulping. He was sweating beneath his surgical mask. "I'm sorry… uh… you scared me. I'm afraid I can't tell you much yet. Maybe… maybe you could help me, assuming you were the one that found him? Is there anything you can tell me about the accident?"

"The idiot was putting spurs on that pet roadrunner of his," she told the doctor. "I heard the noise from the other room. I don't like to pry in his stupid affairs. But, I went to look and there he was, covered in blood and feathers, the *pendejo*. That painted chicken is lucky it jumped out of the window before I got there. Such a mess. I'll be cleaning that room for a week."

"Well, um, I will take that into consideration in my report," Dr. Marx said through his surgical mask. He hadn't removed it because he felt it was some filter, some protection against the volatile woman. "With that, uh, information, this report… It shouldn't take long. I will certainly call you at home once I'm finished."

"I'll wait here," she said. Not once had Olga looked at the body of her husband despite his form frozen in agony not a few feet from her. The scowling woman turned her bulky frame and silently went into the waiting room.

Dr. Marx breathed a sigh of relief and leaned against the cool refrigerator, slightly envying the man inside it.

"Hurry, doctor," a voice whispered. "She'll be back any minute."

Dr. Marx's eyes shot open and darted around the room. There was nothing amiss, no table overturned or apparition standing in the corner. "Good god, man," Dr. Marx said to himself and found a clean sponge to wipe his forehead. "Now you're hearing things. Get it together. She's just a human being. Just a scary, scary human being." After a few deep breaths, the doctor went to thoroughly examine the wound. He wheeled the crane-like lamp over to the table and shined it onto Nestor Piña's face.

In the light, the cuts, the open throat, shimmered for an instant like a television static. Dr. Marx blinked at the corpse and stared at the wound again, but the phenomenon of light didn't reoccur. The doctor decided it was a mirage, a temporary failing of his nerves from the presence of Olga Piña, and went on. Indeed, there were three jagged cuts across his throat and scratches across his chin and chest. All of it looked consistent with a large bird mauling a man while wearing spurs. But, on closer inspection, he noticed something wasn't right. Something he couldn't quite see though he knew it was there.

Nestor Piña's head turned with startling speed. "She's coming! Say nothing or I will curse you!" the corpse hissed despite the torn throat. Then, as quickly as he'd come to life, the brujo resumed the face of hopeless agony at the hands of one's own stupidity.

Before Dr. Marx could even react, a heavy stomping sound came from the entrance of the corridor. At that moment, Dr. Marx was unsure of which horrid thing to fear most, the talking corpse of the approaching woman. Olga made the choice simple by her immediate and vocal presence.

"You said this would be quick," she grunted. "Put him in a bag so I can bury the fool. I'm tired of looking at your stupid magazines."

Dr. Marx chanced a glance at Nestor's body and stuttered, "M-M-Mrs. Piña… I've got to ask you to leave. This is… uh… a medical procedure and I… uh… can't have you coming in here and ruining my report. This's got to be thorough."

Olga narrowed her bulging eyes and snarled, though it very well could've been her breathing like an old dog. "Stupid doctors," she grunted while turning to the corridor. "I told you what happened. And it's like cleaning out a chicken. Any old ranchera can do that," she said, pointing to Nestor on the table. Her footsteps echoed through the thin walls of the place as did the creak of a wooden chair in the waiting room.

With the door closed, Dr. Marx stared at the man's body and laughed to himself.

What's with that Roadrunner Down by the Bus Station?

"You're a braver man than me," Nestor Piña said as he pushed himself up on the table. "I can't laugh when that rhinoceros is within a mile of me. She can sense it and she's like an old god: you don't want their attention, no sir," the brujo went on, despite his gaping neck, and oblivious to Dr. Marx, who was stiff and vaguely stuttering at the sight of the dead man sitting up. When Nestor Piña noticed the doctor's posture, he motioned for the man to calm down.

"I was joking about the curse thing," Nestor said. "I just wanted you to know I'm serious--"

"You-you-you're dead," Dr. Marx stuttered.

Nestor looked at the panicked doctor and scoffed. "Come here," he said. He gestured for him to come closer. As if in a trance, the doctor came forward. Nestor took Dr. Marx's hand and placed it on his wounded neck.

Dr. Marx tried to pull away but found that though his hand was visibly touching garish tears in flesh, it felt like an intact throat. The brujo let him go after that.

"You were about to see it," Nestor said. "Couldn't have you telling my wife I'm not really dead. It took this long for me to even pull it off. I swear, Erronymous is a genius."

"Erronymous?" Dr. Marx asked. He looked around the room as if expecting whatever was linked to the name would pop out and devour him.

"Yeah, my roadrunner," Nestor said, cracking his neck.

"Olga said he killed you," Dr. Marx said. "Cut you when you put spurs on--"

"I *know* the story," Nestor said, winking. "Just goes to show none of you know a damn thing about my craft. The bird and I are bound together. Erronymous is my familiar, my demon-link to The One Beneath the Flames. Right now, he's in a town called San Casimiro or on his way at least. I'm meeting him by bus."

"What? W...," Dr. Marx stammered. "Why would he meet you--"

"Instead of go with me?" Nestor scoffed, shaking his head. "So much for being a smart guy, eh? I guess all the degrees on the wall don't teach you that you can't take a roadrunner on the bus. And Erronymous won't stand for getting stuffed in a suitcase. Thing came from the place where madness dwells and torment is the food on which they gorge, but he refuses to get in a suitcase for three hours. But—" Nestor started then looked at the door as though Olga was standing there. "Sorry. Goddamn, that woman scares the shit out of me." He noticed the doctor's frantic eyes and scoffed. "Haven't figured it out yet? I'm breaking out. Busting loose. After today, I'll finally be free."

"From who?" Dr. Marx found himself asking.

"The one who goes bump in the night," Nestor whispered, pointing to the hall with his thumb. "That behemoth sitting in the waiting room. This whole sham, all of it is to get away from her. Oh, don't think this is the first thing I've tried," the brujo said. "Poisoned her twice. Poison from the breasts of the Infernal Whore, and all it did was give her gas so bad it made *me* want to pull out my eyes and clog my nose with them--which I can do. It's nothing with the powers granted to me. But… that woman. I even sent tiny assassins, spiders from the darkest corners of hell, but she picked them off like ticks."

"How is that--"

"There are some things in this world that are forces," Nestor Piña said. "Things that will not be commanded but will only burn everything around them. Olga, oh… even before I sold my soul, I could sense her as if she had that kind of gravity. A lingering pull of something too big to ever understand. Only in the presence of The One Who Dwells Beneath the Flames have I felt such power. But… my master uses me for his own ends… she…," he said, breaking off. He looked around as though checking to make sure Olga wasn't nearby. "She used me like an experiment in cruelty, a test of her own twisted imagination. At first, they were the little tortures of married life. The giving up of my everyday pleasures. The time spent away from my calling. But, as the years went by, each on seemed to make her crueler for the sake of cruelty. The One Who Dwells Beneath the Flames was created for such things, but she freely chose them… and mastered them."

"If you can… can produce visions," Dr. Marx said. "If you have the power, why not--"

"She is a *force*," Nestor reminded the man. "The power my frame can hold can barely keep up with such a monster. But, if you'll help me, I can get out of this place. Get away from her."

"How can I?" Dr. Marx asked more out of reflex than logic. All of it, Olga and the talking corpse, the conspiring bird, and the gaping wound, had his mind reeling.

"Just sign that paper," Nestor said and pointed at the papers on the rolling tray. "Then, tell my wife that you can't fix up my neck without it looking like a horror movie. Suggest a closed casket or, hell, tell her to roast me. She'll go home, I'll go dance my way to the bus station."

"I can't," Dr. Marx said, thinking of Olga's bloated eyes. "She'll see right through me."

"Yes, you can," Nestor scoffed. "Trust me buddy, if she doesn't think I'm dead, she'll be after me, not you. It's simple. Get her in here, get her out. That's all."

The doctor didn't say anything for a while.

"Look at you after five minutes with her," Nestor said. "I've got twenty years on you. Hell, after two years, I went into the *monte* naked except for javalina blood painted on my chest. An eternity of hell fire will be like oils sprinkled on my head. Let me lie down and then call her in." The brujo swung his legs onto the table and resumed the position he'd rehearsed in the shed for months. "Game time," he whispered as he twisted his face into that of frozen agony it held before.

Dr. Marx looked at Nestor Piña and blinked, briefly wondering if all of it hadn't've been some evidence that his mind was failing. But, all the same, he poked his head out of the examination room and called out to Olga, "Mrs. Piña, I'm done with my report. You... you may view your husband now," he said to the corridor though he couldn't see her.

After a moment, something moved in the waiting room, lumbering onto its feet.

When he heard the stomping, Dr. Marx shot back into the examination room, rushing to his paperwork for the excuse to not meet the woman's eyes.

Olga Piña came into the room as though she smelt fear there. "What did you find?" she asked, walking up to Nestor.

"It… it was as you said," Dr. Marx said. "His throat was cut with a sharp instrument. The lacerations are consistent with a bird attack, too."

Olga listened to him explain the technicalities and medical jargon without emotion. "So, he's dead and there is nothing left to do?" she asked after Dr. Marx had finished talking.

"I'm afraid so," Dr. Marx muttered, nervously stealing glances at the frozen form of Nestor Piña. "And… uh… excuse my suddenness, but I can't patch up that neck wound without it looking just awful. It's just a bit beyond my expertise. I'd have to suggest a closed casket, maybe even cremation. All of which… I provide for a modest fee, unless you've--"

Olga Piña bent over the body of her husband. She stared at him for a long time, snorting satisfied sounds to herself. "Put him in an oak casket," she told the doctor. "Bare oak. It's what the prophets used to seal away the false idols. You know what that means, Nestor?" she asked her husband. "I'll get old and happy and you'll be trapped with splinters in your ass." She spat in the corpse's face and snorted one of her satisfied sounds, then turned to leave the room.

Dr. Marx watched her with growing relief. Yes, the horrid woman, barring his knowledge of Nestor's plan, had spat into the twisted face of her dead husband and cursed him. But, once she left the office, once she drove her old pickup to the outskirts of Calles de Lodo, Nestor could leave and Dr. Marx could fill an oak casket with rocks and bury it in the St. Boniface Cemetery. After that, the next time Dr. Marx would deal with Olga Piña personally would be at her own autopsy.

Olga Piña stopped at the door, turned, and said, "But, on second thought, perhaps cremation would be better. More cost efficient."

"That would be fine, indeed," Dr. Marx said and nodded. "I'll take care of it myself. I assure you, the remains and vessel will be exquisite." When she didn't move immediately, the doctor laughed to break the tension but only served in agitating his parched vocal chords.

"Do you have the machine here?" Olga asked him.

"Yes," Dr. Marx said. "We do everything in-house."

"I'd like to watch," Olga said without blinking. "It will help me… grieve," she went on. Dr. Marx felt that, beneath the weight of her cheeks, Olga Piña was smiling. "And the urn will still be made of oak," she added.

54

"I-I will have to prepare the body first," Dr. Marx said. "The furnace room is down the hall, last door on the right."

"No need to clean him up or strip him," she said. "I hated that shirt on him, best he wear it for eternity." When she got to the door, Olga turned and said, "Don't make me wait long."

Dr. Marx waited until he heard the furnace room's door open before speaking. "What are you going to do?" the doctor asked the frozen corpse of Nestor Piña. When the twisted face of the Brujo of Calles de Lodo didn't twitch, Dr. Marx again wondered if it weren't all some vivid hallucination playing out in front of him.

"I've thought about it," Nestor Piña suddenly said, though his fingers remained clawed and twisted. "Either that mongrel is on to me or she hated me as much as I hated her. Christ! Her spit smells like cheese! But, like I said, I thought it over and... I want you to cook me. Just toss me in that fire--"

"That would kill you!" Dr. Marx said, his hands clapping over his surgical mask in hopes of trapping his loud voice. "Couldn't you just make her *see* your body? This illusion is--"

"Do you think I can snap my fingers and I can make a copy of myself or something?" Nestor asked, shaking his head. "This took me weeks to work out. Weeks of getting all the right ingredients for this. It's just as well... Knowing my luck, she'd find me like she always does. Even if I turned into a frog or something, that'd be the day she'd take up Creole cooking. No, I've had it. I've got friends waiting or me in the fire...Mean ones, but a hell of a lot better than Olga." Nestor Piña laid his head back and sighed. "This is a good thing," he said. "It's good because I'll go somewhere she'll never get me. Trust me, they'd never let her in. Too scary." He resumed his agonized face and ceased moving all together.

"I can't," Dr. Marx argued. "I took an oath to help people. Not to--"

"You *are* helping me," Nestor said. "A few minutes in a fire is nothing compared to how she makes me suffer. Do it, doc."

Dr. Marx stood blinking at the brujo for a while, then went to the end of the rolling examination table and pushed it toward the door. He pushed Nestor Piña to the furnace room. There, Dr. Marx was surprised to see the furnace, always at a state of readiness, was already reaching over one thousand degrees. The furnace looked like a hollowed-out missile with tentacle-like networks of pipes going in and out of it. The grate and round gauges gave it a resemblance to some aquatic mollusk from deep beneath the darkest ocean.

The doctor thought it odd Olga was so eager to help place her husband directly on the steel slab that fed into the fire. Before he pushed the button to retract the steel slab, Dr. Marx let Olga say a few words or any final goodbyes. Instead, she kissed her fingertips and promptly slapped Nestor. "Burn him," he said.

Dr. Marx took one final look at Nestor Piña and pressed the button to start the cremation.

The feet were the first to go, the leather and steel toes scorching and sizzling against skin. With his clothes, Nestor Piña caught faster than expected. Two-foot flames licked at the ceiling from his torso. Even with all this, Nestor Piña dutifully burned as though dead, making Dr. Marx question the entire ordeal. It wasn't until he was in the furnace up to Nestor's ribs that the brujo finally thrashed to life.

Dr. Marx reeled back, trying not only to escape the flames but to put some distance between him and Olga Piña. The ruse was done. The lies unfolded for her to see and the doctor had played a part in it. Lied to her face. Yet, Olga Piña did not so much as look at the doctor. Her eyes were fully on the convulsing body of her husband. Seeing him in flames made her smile as much as her heavy cheeks allow.

If Nestor was aware of his wife's pleasure, it wasn't evident. He was laughing. Despite the skin charring, the eyes boiling, and teeth popping, Nestor Piña howled and laughed.

He was free.

—ETC.—

A Pig Named Orrenius

Patient #132117: Felipe "Pepe" Truchado
Overseeing Physician: Dr. Geronimo Diaz
Transcript of Audio Recording AR0091-LO
Session 8

Q.

Patient #132117:

"Yeah, I know who you are. Doctor Geronimo Diaz. The orderlies all call you Jerry. Today is Wednesday. Howard's president until they impeach him... Why do you always start these things this way? It makes me feel like you think I'm some kind of drooling geek or something."

Q.

Patient #132117:

"Don't pop us so full of pills that we can't think straight, then. That'll fix your *disorientation* right quick. And, like I keep saying, I'm not crazy. Not by a long shot. I don't care what the police told you. My mind's clear as the summer sky. I just want that on the record."

Q.

Patient #132117:

"Yeah, and my wife, god bless her, thinks a stray cigarette cherry can burn down a cinder-block house. She's the
love of my life, but... curing cancer is not in her future, if
you get my meaning."

Q.

Patient #132117:

"It wasn't her I was attacking. I don't care what you've
been told. I wasn't *berserk* or suffering some fit of psy-
chosis. Admittedly, I was acting a little off, but anyone
would've done the same, given the circumstances. Not trying
to say any of it, start to finish, was normal or justified.
Downright bizarre, really. I'll give you that. All I'm saying
is that they were the decisions of a *sane* man just during
insane circumstances."

Q.

Patient #132117:

"What? I'm not agitated. What makes you think I'm
agitated?"

Q.

Patient #132117:

"I pound my fist on my knee for emphasis. Just a habit.
I got it from my father. But, since I can see you getting a
little jumpy, I'll put my hands right here by my sides. See?
All better."

Q.

Patient #132117:
    "You're very welcome, doc."

Q.

Patient #132117:
    "The pig. You want to talk about the pig. It's the reason I'm enjoying your institution's fine hospitality. Nothing but horsemeat and sour milk. But, yes, I know you want to hear about the pig."

Q.

Patient #132117:
    "I wouldn't go saying his name all willy-nilly like that, doc. I wasn't a superstitious man before all this, but I certainly didn't go necking in any graveyards, if you know what I mean."

Q.

Patient #132117:
    "Doc, you can think I'm silly for being terrified of it, but you don't understand is all. I saw it for what it was. What it *really* was. Any *sane* man would be scared shitless."

Q.

Patient #132117:
    "In Dodd, Texas. Little slaughterhouse town. You can smell it from San Marcos. That's where I first ran into the pig."

Q.

Patient #132117:

"There you go tempting fate again. Well, don't come looking for me when he leaves your brain reeling like a rape
victim and you need someone to believe *you*. All you'll get
is 'I told you so' out of me."

Q.

Patient #132117:

"Just from looking at it, there wasn't a thing about it
that was all that special. It was a little bigger than some.
A black spot on its head and three legs with black sock
patches."

Q.

Patient #132117:

"There at the local slaughterhouse. Liendo's Quality
Meat Processing Inc. The boss, that prick, demoted me when
he caught me sneaking a few beers during lunch. He can
think what he likes, but any Truchado that's worth his name
can drink two tall-boys in an hour and still work the con-
veyor. But, he moved me out to the Checkpoint."

Q.

Patient #132117:

"That's what we call the outdoor chutes. They were all
twists and turns just like at the airport checkpoints. Well,
that and because you can't just let a shipment of swine go tearing through a slaughterhouse. They are sanitary. Kind of have
to be by law... unlike some psychiatric facilities it seems.

"But, you got to look for any that are sick and paint them with a marker so the guys working the doors can send them to the furnace. Chalk it up as a loss and call the distributor to cuss them out. Pretty standard, but it's all day in the sun and there ain't a cloud in Dodd. Not one. By the end of the day, you've got to peel the gloves off and slither out of your clothes like a snake. I used to line my seats with trash bags just to keep the smell off, not that it helped much.

"Had I known I'd've been working at Liendo's, I would've sprung for the leather interior.

"But, the stink in your car and blood on your clothes wasn't the worst of working the Checkpoint. The damnedest thing about it--I mean enough to drive a man insane--was the smell. Nothing but a quarter acre of slick pig shit baking in the sun. And do you know what a pig eats? *Anything.* Trash and rotten food and dead mice and other pig's shit and mud and god damn anything. Then, all that comes blasting out when they're nervous, like say when they get off an interstate trip to a place where all they hear is pigs getting cut up.

"They can smell the blood, you know. They know it's their own."

Q.

Patient #132117:

"Pigs are smarter than you think."

Q.

Patient #132117:

"Like I said, he didn't look like much at first. And, please stop using his name. I get that it's all a joke to you, but I can tell you what that pig really is… and it's nothing to go calling on."

Q.

Patient #132117:
"Walls or no walls, he can hear us."

Q.

Patient #132117:
"He was just standing in a corner under a spot with a little shade coming off the crisscrossing posts. He was covering his eyes from the sun. Wasn't moving with the rest of them. See, the pigs are like people. Get them all panicked and they'll follow anyone. To us, action means knowledge, you know. Same with pigs.

"The ones in front bolt into the chutes and the ones in back go thinking the first ones got a plan when, in fact, they're just as scared as the ones in back. Usually, they all move pretty quick. Road trips scare the shit out of them.

"Like I said, they *usually* just run through and that's that. Just got to walk steady behind them and they'll move for you. But, sometimes you get a stubborn one that's spooked frozen. Then, you got to get them moving."

Q.

Patient #132117:
"With a stick."

Q.

Patient #132117:

    "Do I derive any pleasure from striking pigs with a stick? Let me ask you, do you like seeing one of your patients roughed up? Pinned down by some of your nice orderlies and stabbed with a needle?"

Q.

Patient #132117:

    "It *is* the same. Here, you could say we're looney. But, you still think we're people, don't you? You don't like seeing us hurt, I wouldn't think."

Q.

Patient #132117:

    "So then why would I like whacking a pig that's scared about running to the knife? Sure, when I see them that's it. The end of their little piggy lives. Once I'm out of sight, they'll get torn up, made into ribs and sausages and pickled pig's feet and bacon and all that. Everything packaged but the squeal. Doesn't mean I've got to make the rest of their lives, although short, any worse. They're going to trade their lives so a family don't starve. That's heroic. You got to respect that.

    "Anyway, it was standing there shading its eyes and I got near it, kind of waved my arms around, but it wouldn't move. I made a noise at it, but still, it didn't do a thing. It just looked up at me. Not all jerky like a pig neither. Looked up

at me like an old man lost in his thoughts and barely noticing that I was standing there. For some reason, and this is
going to sound odd, but that pig looked at me like he didn't
think much of me. Like I was beneath him."

Q.

Patient #132117:

"What! How the hell can a pig offend somebody? No, I
didn't get mad. It was just a pig--"

Q.

Patient #132117:

"--or so I thought. After it looked at me like that, I
just took the stick and tapped at its back legs. Get a little jump out of it, but the thing gave the stick a look and
snorted. Again, there was something... I don't want to say
human because it certainly doesn't have anything close to
humanity in it... but, there was something intelligent in
the look."

Q.

Patient #132117:

"Not *that* smart. Not smart enough to know some fool with
a stick ain't going to do him no harm when a slaughterhouse
is looming a few yards away.

"No, that thing looked at the stick, then to me again,
and then shut its eyes. I shook my head and gave him a good
whack on the back, more noise than anything. But, that's
when it got weird.

"I hit him once, then he spun and I jumped back in case
he tried to bite me. Pigs, you know, can take a chunk out of

your leg easy as if it was cheesecake. But, it didn't chomp or squeal, just turned to look me in the face, black eyes all narrowed. I brought the stick up again and started hooting and hollering at it, thinking that would move it. But, like it sensed me about to whack it again, it spoke to me. Not with its mouth or anything. It was..."

Q.

Patient #132117:

"It was like its voice was in my head. Like it was talking directly to my brain."

Q.

Patient #132117:

"It... it said, 'Touch me with that stick again and I'll take it and fuck your dead mother with it until her cunt's nothing but torn lips and splinters.'"

Q.

Patient #132117:

"What do you think I did? Put down the stick, told my boss I needed a break, and got some water. I mean, come on doc, you work my job long enough, you know a touch of the sun can make your head a little foggy. Sometimes it even makes you see things, hear things that aren't there."

Q.

Patient #132117:

"No, I didn't go back there for the rest of the day. Thankfully, a shipment came early and another came in late and, I'll tell you, five hundred unscheduled pigs does plenty to stop production. You can't kill them as fast as they get there. So, we all, the guys in the Checkpoint, went and cleaned up before going into Liendo's and doing our share of the killing."

Q.

Patient #132117:
"Nothing. I wasn't thinking about anything."

Q.

Patient #132117:
"No, it's just I never liked killing pigs. They look at you... I mean so do cows and chickens and all the rest, but like I said, pigs are smart. They smell the blood and hear the squeals from the other room and they know. They'll give you a look like they're wondering why, as if they expect an explanation, but all they get is the axe."

Q.

Patient #132117:
"It's a figure of speech, doc. We don't use axes or sledges anymore. All air guns now."

Q.

Patient #132117:
"I don't know where he was, but I'm sure tucked into some corner somewhere I'm sure. That's what he does, see, what they all do. The demons or whatever they are. They hide

in plain sight. Not in crypts or black masses or haunted houses. They're sitting next to us at the movies, giving us change at the Maverick Market. The only place we don't look is in front of our faces and they know it."

Q.

Patient #132117:

"No, I went home same as any day, though I'll admit I was thinking about that pig. That voice. Sounded old... like someone not of this time trying on English for a while and not liking the fit."

Q.

Patient #132117:

"The real question is, 'why *would* I tell my wife?' God bless her, she doesn't ask for much. She's happy married to a man who comes home smelling like pig-death, leaving little hairs everywhere, attracting all the stray dogs in Dodd. But, a man reeking like the last moments of a pig and going on about how a pig talked to him at work. I love my wife too much to do that to her."

Q.

Patient #132117:

"I didn't try to do anything to her. It was... him."

Q.

Patient #132117:

"The same."

Q.

Patient #132117:

"The next day, we were still dealing with the back-up from the day before and Liendo made sure it was running like a circus. All his clowns dancing and falling after the pigs in the Checkpoint. It was odd. I didn't think much of it at the time. I mean, I was still a little spooked from the day before but I thought it was just one of those days."

Q.

Patient #132117:

"The pigs were acting strange. A little wilder."

Q.

Patient #132117:

"It'll happen on occasion. They get that way if a pack of coyotes comes sniffing around or if the townies get bored and throw rocks at the pens for nothing but a thing to do. But, no, thinking back on it, knowing what I know now, they were just reacting to him. They could tell what he was.

"I'll not say his name and you best not either. Placate me, doc. Please.

"Some of them were almost running into the slaughterhouse. I mean fighting to get in there. The other ones were, I don't know, changed. I'd met mean pigs. A buddy of mine, R.J., got bit right on the hip. Walks like a damn stork now and will until his dying day. Said the pig popped right out of a cluster of them and took a bite. Not a tester neither. No nibble. Like he wanted to eat him whole if he could.

"Still has teeth marks on the bone. Carved right in there."

Q.

Patient #132117:
"I don't think, I know. That's what they do. Realize it or not, but your body, your mind... hell, even your soul feels it. Feels the energy they're giving off. The shit they draw in."

Q.

Patient #132117:
"Bad things, doc. Either the worst in man or more like them."

Q.

Patient #132117:
"No. There wasn't anything else really, other than the thunder."

Q.

Patient #132117:
"Yes, it could've been one of those rare occurrences. Doesn't mean that it is, though."

Q.

Patient #132117:
"The thunder? That day, there was a thunderstorm. And, before you say it, let me tell you why that's so odd.
"It was only around the slaughterhouse.

"I lived miles away, you know, before you offered me a room in this resort. Was a clear sky that day. The dawn colors flaring up as I went my route. Then, there came the turn off 372, the ten mile stretch up to Liendo's, and there it was. A cloud bank that covered all the place and the lots and damn near half of the road.

"Driving up, it was like day and night switching places."

Q.

Patient #132117:

"Yeah, I saw him that day. Near quitting time."

Q.

Patient #132117:

"Liendo didn't give a shit about the thunder clouds or the lightning and all that. Said a schedule's a schedule and that, besides, we had rubber boots and wouldn't get shocked. Never mind we were in a web of ironwork, rubber boots were going to be the things that saved us.

"Anyway, neither you nor the state wants me yammering on about that slave-driving prick. We'd mostly cleared out the clog and it was near quitting time when I spotted him. I recognized the coloration.

"He didn't look at me. Was kind of looking up at the thunderclouds. Didn't know the truth yet, but it was damn weird seeing him, nose up in the air, like he was smelling the electricity."

A Pig Named Orrenius

Q.

Patient #132117:

    "I admit I hesitated at first, but I told myself the voice wasn't anything but the heat and a bad night of drinking mixed together. I went up to him, stick up in the air, hooting.

    "Then he looked at me.

    "Looked at me like he recognized me.

    "'Off to the knife with you!' I told him, trying to get him to move."

Q.

Patient #132117:

    "I wouldn't say I talk to pigs often because I don't consider what I do talking to pigs. When you're around a dog and it barks, you can usually tell its mood, right? But it's not saying 'I'm mad, master. I wish to play.' You get the intent from the sound of it.

    "Same with all animals. I know what I'm saying. I understand the complexity of the thought. Animals just pick up on the intent."

Q.

Patient #132117:

    "I know he understood. He looked past me, right into the chute that runs them into the slaughterhouse where all the folk were tired and counting the minutes, killing sloppy because they were tired and so close to a shower they could already feel the stink of death peeling off them. Oh yeah, he looked at the Liendo's lights and plain refused.

"Gave me a snort and didn't move."

Q.

Patient #132117:

"I went to give it a whack."

Q.

Patient #132117:

"The voice shot back into my head. Said, 'Strike me and know thy doom, you fucking cunt... or aid my escape and know splendors your peasant brain could never imagine... Pepe Truchado.'

"It knew my fucking name.

"It said it like he was dangling my lunch money in front of me. Teasing me. But, that wasn't the worst.

"All the talking, the voice going on and on... I swear it was doing something to me."

Q.

Patient #132117:

"What could I do? I just froze up for a while, but there weren't many pigs left in the Checkpoint. Maybe a dozen. And Esposito was already calling for the last of them."

"Just shook my head and went to get him moving, but then it spoke again."

Q.

Patient #132117:

"He said, 'Name what you want. The things that you secretly stroke yourself to. The things lingering in your perversity... A thousand Peggy Sandovals will defile themselves at your whim... if I do not step foot in there.'"

Q.

Patient #132117:

"A girl I graduated with."

Q.

Patient #132117:

"At the time, she was *the* girl. The one that set my young cock throbbing. She used to wear these striped sweaters to English class that showed off a set that would make you believe in god again. Beat my meat raw for years thinking of those tits.

"That Peggy Sandoval... No one special. But, it's just one of those firsts that stick with you. There aren't that many people who know that name means a thing to me. Let alone a pig.

"But, for the record, I love my wife. Never once so much as smiled at another woman. So, even though that's what he led with, that had nothing to do with it. Nothing."

Q.

Patient #132117:

"Because if you put the rubber stamp on me and keep me in this looney bin, I at least want my wife to be able to say, 'Yeah, Pepe was nuts, but he loved me to death.' Pardon the expression."

Q.

Patient #132117:

"I helped him because he's some kind of devil that's why. I don't care what he looked like. A thing that could do what it did, even that little bullshit at the Checkpoint... that's beyond men. There was a power in him that... that was older than the world. More evil that anything any one of your patients did to get in here. The words in my head were a start. The taste. The next one was the vision."

Q.

Patient #132117:

"Yeah, kind of like a hallucination, I guess. Never did any of those drugs that send you to the edge of space and back. But, I don't think it would be like that at all.

"I got the feeling that I woke up in the middle of another life, full of memories and marks of things I both remembered and knew never happened. I lived a whole day in that new life. Brushed my teeth over a sink that was mine for a decade though I'd never seen it before. Felt a sore shoulder from an old lacrosse injury when I know I've never even heard of the sport. I fucked the wife who was not my wife. Looked at the view in Denver when I've never even seen a picture of it. And it was good. That life he showed me.

"I was rich. Strong. Cock like a mule. Lived that confidence, that arrogance. Went to sleep in my strange bed that just embraced me like I'd slept there a thousand times."

Q.

Patient #132117:

"Yes, that's when I started screaming, when the guys came running to get me and all that."

Q.

Patient #132117:

"I think the pig didn't want to get chopped up and forced twenty-four hours into my brain in less than a millisecond. And that a screaming coworker at twenty minutes 'til quitting time is a good way to stay out of the slaughterhouse for the rest of the day.

"You have to understand, that's all we are to them. Things. Levers and keys and buttons."

Q.

Patient #132117:

"Then, I wasn't sure why he didn't just escape. Pigs'd done it before.

"Now, I know why this demon swine didn't just leave: there's no fun in it. He wanted to torture me. Took an interest in me, you could say. Maybe it was because I threatened to hit him or maybe it's just that I was there."

Q.

Patient #132117:

"Don't think it's personal, doc. It isn't *me* me. It's just the want of a person. Anyone. No matter who you are, you are a network of human connection and with each one is an opportunity to inflict misery on countless others. To inflict torment.

"Like I said, if he hated me and wanted me dead, I'd already be in the ground. But, *near* me, then he gets to run wild on dozens of others."

Q.

Patient #132117:

"The next day, Ricky Sauza died, didn't he? Call it an accident all you want, but I had to *see* it. The pig showed me. Made damn sure I saw it."

Q.

Patient #132117:

"Don't quote the story to me, doc. I know it. I was there. I know a rattlesnake jumped and bit him, that he fell into a bunch of pigs and… they tore him apart. But, if you don't know pigs, it doesn't sound like anything. Just bad luck.

"But, pig men will tell you those hogs'll eat a snake without a thought. They'll fight over it like candy.

"And, like I told you, that snake wasn't any kind I'd ever seen. Had the diamonds, but a little white crescent moon on its head. Didn't rattle neither. Just bit Ricky on the knee and slithered back beneath that demon pig--"

Q.

Patient #132117:
"Doc, I'm really trying not to lose it here. This place already presses every button a sane man has. And, I've already said it. *Please*, please, please, *please*, don't say his name again.
"I don't want to hear you had to bury kinfolk over it.
"I can tell you don't want to believe.
"But, he *made* me a believer with Ricky Sauza."

Q.

Patient #132117:
"He had told me to open the pen doors so he could get out."

Q.

Patient #132117:
"I was going to, believe me, but my first thought wasn't obedience. I thought of my job and my wife. One needed the other and I needed both, you know."

Q.

Patient #132117:
"He growled at me and then squealed a sound that drove the other pigs insane.
"That's when Ricky got bit by that devil snake.
"God damn, I can still see it."

Q.

Patient #132117:

"The frenzy of it... there was a hate to it. Like they didn't want him to die from anything but a bunch of tiny, vicious bites.

"We all just stood there frozen. Every bit of us scared out of our heads, watching Ricky get devoured. He looked at me. Through the pigs and the blood, he looked at me. I knew he was looking from the whites of his eyes. It... it was something that pig wanted me to see. The fear. The undeniable pain and finality of those eyes. Terrified at the understanding that hog heads would be the last thing for them to see.

"When someone reached in and pulled one of his hands, it was just the hand and forearm that came up... and a pig fought for that too."

Q.

Patient #132117:

"No, it was the following night. After Ricky's memorial."

Q.

Patient #132117:

"Yeah, the funeral was a formality the next afternoon. For his mother and kids and all. But, Liendo offered to have the wake at the plant since it had a good-sized mess hall. Surprised the hell out of us that all it took for him to act human was Ricky being eaten alive on the property."

Q.

Patient #132117:

"Thank you. And, no, the pig wasn't present, not like Sauza's wife was anyway. Didn't pass out tissues when Liendo put a picture of him up next to the old TV set bolted to the wall. But, the pig was there sure as he is here now."

Q.

Patient #132117:

"He's right behind you, doc."

Q.

Patient #132117:

"Oh, he's there all right. He's there and in the hallway and my room and the guard station and outside of here too. He is where we go and always will be."

Q.

Patient #132117:

"The voice was what did it.

"In the middle of his cousin giving one hell of a toast to Ricky, there was a voice from the back of the room. It was loud and mean and it was saying things like 'Your little whore boy belongs to us now, you filthy cunts!' and 'He takes to his sodomies like a hungry babe suckling at a hag's teat!' Horrible things.

"I spun around, ready to fight whoever the fuck would say such things, expected half the room to be... but, it was like I was the only one that heard it. My wife just thought I was, I don't know, grieving or something and squeezed my hand tighter. And it just kept on and on.

"'He drowns not in the rivers but fire and the seed of hellspawn! Cleaved in two by swords of meat and bone!' it went. Really vicious shit.

"I dropped my wife's hand and followed it. The barking sound of it...

"I... I looked over at the window. It was all black and reflective from the glare of the lights and dark outside. The pig's face came out of nowhere. Just out of the dark to look in my eyes not like some animal that squeezed under a fence and sniffed out the carrot cake, but like a thing, something cruel, wearing the body of a pig."

Q.

Patient #132117:

"I told my wife I needed some air and, like the saint she is, she said she understood."

Q.

Patient #132117:

"Nothing was by that window. Not so much as a track or anything."

Q.

Patient #132117:

"Just because I found him in the pens doesn't mean he wasn't there at the window, doc. That stuff might impress us, but something like that--projection, you know--isn't shit to that pig. It sent the world worse in his time, much worse than that."

Q.

Patient #132117:

"Other than the fact that when I got close enough to the pens to see, he was alone. The only thing was that he was looking me dead in the face. And not like some dumb brute, but like a gator watching a crane get too close. A kind of, I don't know... sinister satisfaction."

Q.

Patient #132117:

"Yes, but you don't have to say it in that tone."

Q.

Patient #132117:

"He told me to come back before dawn to get him out. He said he would not be put in that slaughterhouse."

Q.

Patient #132117:

"No, doc. You see, a common thug says he'll kill your family or something like that. The pig and his kind, they do things that are far more effective.

"The things he made me watch... The images...

"Horrible things done by creatures I know don't have a human name... My wife... my mother and father..."

Q.

Patient #132117:

"I don't know. Less than a second. Anymore, I think, and I'd've had a stroke."

Q.

Patient #132117:

"Went back in to the memorial service and force-fed myself a sliver of pecan pie so no one would think anything of me. Then, went home and told my wife I just didn't think I could sleep and, bless her heart, she just kissed me on the head and went off to bed.

"She was out by eleven."

Q.

Patient #132117:

"She takes sleeping pills. Well, halves anyway. The full ones mess with her memory."

Q.

Patient #132117:

"The next day was Sunday, well, it was Sunday––I took off at twelve-o-one. Went as fast as I could so I wouldn't get a ticket."

Q.

Patient #132117:

"That was different. When I thought of getting fired, that was for my family's sake. Getting a ticket or arrested would mean that *he* would have to wait. As long as you're thinking of him, he seemed to let it slide."

Q.

Patient #132117:

"I saw him. Twice. On the corner of Bellevue and Jacinto, standing on the corner, the people hanging around, smoking cigarettes and laughing, like a four hundred pound pig wasn't standing right there with them.

"The second time was at Snyder Hill. You know that steep climb and that rollercoaster tip. That kid crossing sign, the one with the reflective tape, it caught in my headlights like Dodd intended, but beneath it...

"He was looking at me with those black eyes, those ears flopped over like ram-horns... he was there in the light, then he was gone. Lost in the shadows of the ditch-grass."

Q.

Patient #132117:

"At Liendo's, I parked outside the gate. Liendo's got the only key and he's there at six a.m. six days a week sick or raining or come the Tribulations. Don't think it was out of kindness or a feeling of responsibility. That asshole thought if we ever got a set, we'd go in there and rob him blind. Like there's a big market for air-guns and old wheelbarrows we use to cart around the bodies after the steam bath."

Q.

Patient #132117:

"Let my truck roll up against the gate. Chain popped."

Mario E. Martinez

Q.

Patient #132117:

"I pulled up to the pens. They were unusually noisy for that time of night. Like when he got them to kill Ricky, and, like before, he was there alone, all the other pigs were fighting over themselves to get away from him.

"He was looking at me, the headlights making it seem like his eyes were glowing green. It gave me the idea that he'd been waiting for me.

"Getting him out wasn't a problem. The gate's nothing but a simple snap and chain-lock. When I opened it, none of the other pigs even tried to get out. Most times, a pig that's been penned long enough'll try to wedge its way out of anything bigger than a rat hole. No. Only one to trot out was *him*. He passed and snorted at me like I was some incompetent manservant."

Q.

Patient #132117:

"Not a word. Didn't say a thing, just went and circled my truck. I didn't bother locking the gate since I didn't want that demon pig thinking I was prioritizing Liendo's property over him. But, I hunted up a sturdy plank of wood and let down the tailgate. Set them up so he could walk right up into the bed...

"He didn't like that. Not one bit."

Q.

Patient #132117:

"In that instant, I was in another body again. A slave to some kind of king the likes of which I'd never seen. All gold

and rings and dark eyes and painted lines. He was whipping me to death. The end of the cat-o-nines tipped with
obsidian chips and snake fangs. Felt my eyes get slashed
like balloons and my sight go oozing out from my sockets
in rivers. Felt the stones chip against my ribs, the veins
tearing. Then, I was back at my truck.

"I was weeping, grabbing at my eyes to make sure Liendo's
wasn't just some dream in a darkness that would be forever."

Q.

Patient #132117:

"I told him I was sorry, then opened the passenger door
for him. Tried to lift him, but he bit at me and said, 'Your
innocent hands are undeserving of touching even this vessel's flesh.' So, I got the plank and made a little ramp that
led into the cab.

"I was afraid it would break and that then he'd *really*
get mad, but it held and he got in the seat. Sat in it like he
was a dog or something."

Q.

Patient #132117:

"Went to a Maverick Market. The one over on Dober
Street. Wanted to gas up and use the hose to wash off the
tires. Figured, if Liendo thought someone broke in and
opened the gates, well, their tires would have mud on them,
you know. The pens run so rampant with piss and shit, the
whole lot around it is permanently muddy. But, the parking
lot is pavement. So, if I showed up with messy tires, Liendo
might catch on.

"He agreed with me, I guess. He didn't instruct me to do
anything except not touch him... like I wanted to."

Q.

Patient #132117:
"I don't *claim* it. That's what happened."

Q.

Patient #132117:
"I'll say it again so you when you give this report over to the sheriff, he'll know my side of it and he'll see it doesn't change. Not once. So, let me say it again: I didn't kill Drew Spencer. I was washing the tires off, leaving *the pig's* side for last. I didn't want him looking at me again, not with those eyes. And, as I was spraying a tire down, I noticed that the pig wasn't looking at me anymore, but at the convenience store. And, when I say looking, I mean just glaring at it.

"I turned around and there was Drew, looking at us from inside the store.

"He had his face pressed against the glass doors looking out at me... like there wasn't anyone there. Like he was some lifeless puppet. He... he had something in his hands. At first, I didn't know what it was, but then I saw it was a pair of shears... I saw them when he started stabbing himself in the neck. Over and over. Blood splattering the glass and pooling beneath the door.

"His hands got so slick with blood he must've dropped the shears or maybe the pig told him to, I don't know. But, he took his finger, dabbed at the wound, and started writing on the glass. It was no language I'd ever seen... but, even then, I swore I could almost read it. Then Drew started pounding his head against the doorframe. Hard. Damn near shook the doors off the hinges.

"I dropped the hose and went to my driver's side, but, I caught eyes with him, with that pig. 'Clean the tires, you pussy, and then watch,' he told me."

Q.

Patient #132117:

"I cleaned the last tire and stood there watching Drew--face white as paper from the lack of blood--smash his skull on the doorframe until it was concave. He hit his head so hard it broke his neck. You could hear it from where we were. Through the glass. It was like an old tree branch snapping.

"But, head dangling, Drew kept at it. Kept up the pounding until we were gone. For all I know, he never stopped."

Q.

Patient #132117:

"At least he got to die. Sure, goddamn brutal as it was, he didn't have to live it for long. I'd say even *that* kind of death is preferable to all this, but I know if I did, then you'd put me in the Rubber Room again."

Q.

Patient #132117:

"What's to like about it? There's nothing in it but a drain to shit in. The nutrition-balls you make us eat. And, it's not like I'm ever alone in there.

"He's always there. Waiting."

Mario E. Martinez

Q.

Patient #132117:

"It's hard to explain, doc. I was trying *not* to think of anything, no one or no place. I had the feeling that if he caught me thinking about my wife, that's where he'd want to go so he could rape her and bite out her throat in front of me.

"I was just driving around, radio off, and windows down.

"It was during this time that I started thinking I was losing it. That pig... he was just sitting there, head out the window, and ears flapping in the wind. He looked like a pig. Smelled like a pig. But, when I was looking at him... I don't know, he must've felt it because he turned to me and narrowed his eyes.

"'Take me to the whores,' he told me."

Q.

Patient #132117:

"I didn't ask what he wanted the prostitute for. Maybe they'd be easiest to get to or no one would miss them. I don't know and, truth be told, I didn't want to know. If those pictures in my head were an inkling of what that pig could do, I didn't want to think about what it could do to a woman whose very business is being vulnerable.

"No, I just swung the car towards Chavez Park."

Q.

Patient #132117:

"That's where the working girls hang out."

A Pig Named Orrenius

Q.

Patient #132117:

"Friend told me. Hey! Don't give me that look!

"I've never touched another woman in my married life, understand? Knowledge of sin doesn't make me a sinner, does it?"

Q.

Patient #132117:

"Like I said, it's where they hang out. So, I didn't drive past it for but a minute before I saw a cluster of them. Maybe four or so. Two booked it when my lights hit them and another took one look into my truck, at my face and at the pig in the passenger seat and left.

"The other one... the last one... don't even want to know her story if she didn't mind the thought of a three-way with a fucking pig. I tell you, doc, the world, am I right? Kind of place that makes you wonder the point of getting out of bed. Nothing but disappointment and women screwing barnyard animals so they can buy a beer and a sandwich... makes you sick if you think about it long enough."

Q.

Patient #132117:

"She came to the window, saying, 'Well, *sooie*, baby. What you looking for tonight?'

"'I'm not looking,' I told her. 'The pig is.'"

Q.

Patient #132117:

"She told me it would cost forty for me, two hundred for the pig. Three hundred for me and the pig. She thought it was funny, looking at him all glassy eyed, yellow teeth showing... You could tell she'd been pretty once. Before it all. You could, I don't know, see it in her smile. Like, once, a long time ago, she used to smile and laugh that way.

"Can you believe that? A woman, someone's daughter--"

Q.

Patient #132117:

"She stopped laughing quick. The pig... he just lunged at her. Snapped at her. I mean went from gentle pig to killer in a split second. He let out a squeal that made the air in my lungs freeze up and blood to come out of my nose. Couldn't see what happened since his bulk got in between us, but she pulled away screaming, nose bit clean off.

"She fell back, her heels getting all wobbly and her ankles jelly... Started running as fast as she could into the *monte* around the park. But, the pig had got a taste and bolted after her. He jumped and cleared the window. I thought he'd tip over, you know, flip right out of the truck. That demon pig, though, he shot out of there like an arrow and landed on all fours like a cat. Took off after her, chasing her into the dark."

Q.

Patient #132117:

"I stayed in the truck... I didn't want him to think I was bothering him. If he'd do those things to me for annoyance, imagine what he'd do for outright defiance."

A Pig Named Orrenius

Q.

Patient #132117:

"He chased her into the brush. Then came the noises. Her screaming in terror and the pig making sounds... like it was really enjoying itself. All the bushes were shaking, hissing like snakes. The pig must've caught her. A big yelp came out of the dark, then a plop. A body hitting the dirt. She was screaming again, telling him to stop, calling for help from god or anyone who would listen. Next came the grunts. The happy pig sounds matched with her hisses of pain and little sobs... I don't know if it was just that loud or if *he* wanted me to hear it, but I heard her saying, 'Please. Stop. I don't want to. Stop. Please,' and then the sounds of him pumping away at her.

"Once he was done, he let out another one of those squeals and I nearly vomited. She was... she was still crying, all that bravado gone, gobbled up by that fucking pig. He could've let her go then. Could've been satisfied with just that, but... that pig. Nothing'll ever be enough."

Q.

Patient #132117:

"There was a loud crunch, then the crying stopped."

Q.

Patient #132117:

"I know he killed her, which made the next part even worse...

"The pig came trotting out of the brush, nose and chest all covered in blood and... she walked out right behind him. Her throat was torn open. All the flesh around it was in ribbons. From her missing nose down, it was just a smear of blood and meat with her yellow teeth peeking through. The clothes were all but torn off. Tits bitten and ruined. Her denim shorts torn off one leg and her busted up parts gleaming in the lamp light.

"She came up to the window again and put her head in the truck--"

Q.

Patient #132117:

"Yes, that's how her blood got in my car. I keep telling you. *I* didn't kill anyone. It was the pig, goddamn it! The pig! Don't you think if I'd done it, there'd only be a couple of drops in there? You saw the pictures, I'm sure. If it was me, I'd still me washing the blood out of my hair."

Q.

Patient #132117:

"She spoke, but in *his* voice. She said, 'Got to get more holes to fuck now since *these* are ruined.' She was laughing again, but now it was like a machine programmed to laugh. She just kept throwing her head back, showing me her ruined neck. I could see the roof of her mouth clear through her lower jaw.

"She laughed and then opened the door. Carried him in. When she did, I heard the bones cracking from the weight, but... the dead don't care, I guess. 'Find us a nice spot,' he told me. 'There's a show coming.'"

Q.

Patient #132117:

    "Found a spot in the dark. Dead as she was, she found a lamppost and leaned against it awkwardly, like she was walking on stilts. Then, we waited."

Q.

Patient #132117:

    "Waited for the show he was talking about."

Q.

Patient #132117:

    "He made that puppet hide her face, hide her ruined chest in the shadow thrown by the light. Got her to stick her leg out so the next guy trolling could see the goods, I suppose. And we didn't have to wait long for someone."

Q.

Patient #132117:

    "If you say so. I didn't know his name. But, Mr. Farias, I guess, pulled up alongside the curb and called out to her. Said he liked her look and he had money to spend. 'Ass and mouth, in that order, honey,' he said and I couldn't see too well, but I know he was waving a stack of bills at her.

    "When she came into the light, that guy hit the pedal to the metal. Got so scared that he ran into the bus stop not far from them. That's where she got him. Dove in the car, got it rocking all right. Nothing but a rocking Buick and his screams and her groans and bites, his headlights shining into the *monte* and made it look like a place alien to me, to reality.

"It looked like all we've ever feared about the dark made horribly real."

Q.

Patient #132117:

"He was watching. Just watching. Little grunts here and there. But, he gave me the impression that he wasn't so much watching as he was experiencing, you know. Like he'd thrown himself into that dead woman and wore her like a costume. She was just a vessel, as he said, and it was one for violence. Nothing more. He was just hunting for a joyride and she was some car left idle in a parking lot.

"Pretty soon, the car stopped shaking and it got real quiet. Could only hear his wet breathing and my engine. She started hitting the glass then. The back window was still in shadow but I heard her clawing at it. The wet skin on the glass...

"'Turn on the lights, see what that shredded cunt's got to show you,' the pig said inside my head.

"I did it. Popped on the headlights.

"Her face was even more horrible, if it could get any worse. There were... pieces of Farias still in her teeth, but it looked like she'd bitten through her own lips to get to the soft flesh of his face. And next to her face was that writing again. The same one--least it seemed to me--that Drew Spencer scribbled onto the glass door.

"The pig told me to read it and I told him I couldn't.

"'Yes, you can,' he told me. 'And, if you do, I will show you things... things only I've seen.' The tone, it got me worried. He'd been the most awful bastard about everything. Wouldn't even sit in the bed of the truck even though it had more air and room. So, imagine that kind of vibe the whole damn time we're together then he starts talking to me softly. Gives me the junior prom voice. Like he knew I wanted to be able to read it, but knew something about it was wrong.

"'All you have to do is try,' he told me. 'And, if you don't, I'll fuck you like I fucked that whore, make you walk around, dead and rotting, right up to your mother so you can shove your rotten cock up her ass.'

"After a minute, I asked him what it was.

"He told me it was his name. That saying it would bind us, link our souls to one another like we shared a secret shame. With it, he and I would share a power that could bend all reality to our will. All I had to do was read it. He said, 'As a sign of good will, I will answer a question of your choosing.'"

Q.

Patient #132117:

"I asked him why, if he had all this power, why he didn't want to go into Liendo's. What was in there that *he* was afraid of? The rest, the tricks I suppose, I'd seen those. But, if he could do that to me, why be scared or even apprehensive about going into a building full of men no smarter than me?"

Mario E. Martinez

Q.

Patient #132117:

"He told me he came from a dark place. A place of fire and no light. Just pain. There was a creature, The One Beneath the Flames, that was the slumbering giant of that realm. Both asleep and brutally alive. The pig was not a pig then. He was in his true shape... goddamn I'll never get that sight out of my head. Like angels had regressed for a million generations until they were like us only in basic shape, but all the features contorted into devices of torture.

"The One Beneath the Flames, he let the pig come into our world centuries ago. So, he could plague humanity with his vileness, he traded his true form for that of a pig's... he bragged about it.

"He's the reason Jews don't eat pork and why Rome burned and the plagues never truly died. There's not one catastrophe in history, no place his cloven hoof hasn't fucked up.

"But, with this new body, the pig had to watch out. He would be cursed to live the lives of his parts until The One Beneath the Flames awoke once more, an eon after the sun went out. If he lost a leg, he'd feel that leg rot no matter how many miles away. Feel it get eaten by maggots and ants until it was clean. He'd feel the pieces as they were divided up by nature, the bone as it degraded into the soil. Agony as each bit of it that was siphoned off by the grass or ground further into the asphalt.

"To be cut up and eaten was to live the eternity of a trillion tortures. To be one and still disjointed. Shat through men like me and flushed to different sides of the state. 'With this vulnerability, I was allowed to enter your world,' he said, 'I am able to both destroy and create according to your wishes... all you must do is read and I can show you...'"

96

Q.

Patient #132117:
"Yes, I read it."

Q.

Patient #132117:
"I won't say it again."

Q.

Patient #132117:
"I saw him for what he was. What he *really* was."

Q.

Patient #132117:
"I don't have the words. And, even if I did, I wouldn't use them. They'd take me right back there again. I'll never forget it, the same way you never forget being afraid as a child. But, you'd never want to go back to that moment. Nothing but the sound of your own blood churning and the world compressing to that horrible thing and then it gets even bigger than the world until you know it will be your destroyer even long after you survived.

"It hurt to look at him. It... it was..."

Q.

Patient #132117:
"I know that tone, doc. The loons in here scream about it until the happy pills put their asses to sleep. You think

this is some whacky vision brought on by my mother running off on me or when I used to get my lunch money stolen at school.

"If you ever find him, don't pretend you're better than me. If you think he's just a pig, that's the last mistake you'll ever make.

"He can do things to you that the worst minds on the planet, in *history*, couldn't even think of in a lifetime."

Q.

Patient #132117:

"What he did to me... what got me here... there's a special kind of hell for a man who would do such a thing, but he just did it for kicks. To break the tedium of eternity. It's one thing to do it for out of infernal service, I suppose... but the pig does it for enjoyment. Pure and simple."

Q.

Patient #132117:

"After I spoke his name, after he showed me the shape he had when he made a deal with The One Beneath the Flames, I tried to keep my eyes shut. Tried to keep the vision of that thing sitting beside me in the cab. Yet, they starting to open and look around.

"I wanted them shut, kept trying to shut them, but my eyes wouldn't listen. My hands went to the gearshift and put the truck in drive. It was then that I realized what was happening. He was wearing me now. Moving my feet and turning my head and working my lungs, starting them and stopping them until my head filled with panic. Then he'd let them fill up with air again, laughing in my head. He was doing to me what he'd done to that poor girl, but I wasn't dead. I wish I had been.

"The feeling is terrible, doc. Like you're in a runaway car. All you can do is watch as you go this way and that way and for all your screaming and pleading, there's nothing you can do. It's that hopelessness, that feeling of utter and complete weakness that's the scariest. I didn't know what to do but scream, but my mouth wouldn't budge except to click my teeth as though to check their strength.

"Driving around town, he looked for some other victim and I wished I could tell my wife that I loved her. I regretted it that instant."

Q.

Patient #132117:

"What I thought, he knew. The second I pictured her, my body started laughing and the pig started grunting. Then I heard myself saying, 'Let's go see that lovely wife of yours. After that piece in the park, I can't go back to the sows. Not tonight!' He swung the truck around and made his way to my house."

Q.

Patient #132117:

"Doc, it's like you haven't been listening. Why would he want to hurt my wife? You're still looking for reasons? You can't just logic your way into understanding them any more than you can stop a burning building with arguments.

"There is no reason to their actions. All they want is every last ounce of our shame, our dignity, and our sanity. When those are gone and no one else listens to us, they'll fuck the corpses and move on.

"I was no more important to him than your socks are to you. When I start getting holes and tears, he'll find another one."

Q.

Patient #132117:

"She was asleep when he parked the truck, I remember that. All the lights were off except the porch light. I tried to honk the horn, tried to scream to warn her, but he only let me feel like it was about to happen. Just a little more anger, a little more *umph,* and she'd be safe. But, I know now that no matter how much I could've tried, he would've kept me at the threshold. Inches away might as well be miles away until you're right there..."

Q.

Patient #132117:

"He was laughing in my head. Laughing like a cruel child."

Q.

Patient #132117:

"She was in bed, TV on but turned down. He stood there, making me watch him watch her. He started rubbing at my crotch, tugging at it as we looked at her... I wanted to kill him then. Wanted to take a rock and smash his pig skull open and cut him up into those thousand pieces so that he could suffer like I was suffering. But, all that was just fuel for the fire.

"The more I thought of revenge, the more my imagination defied him, the stronger he got.

"He made me sit down on the bed next to her. Made me stroke her hair and kiss her cheeks until she woke up and I heard his voice saying, 'She's got quite the body under those pajamas.' And I kept telling him to stop, to leave her alone. Told him I'd trade everything if he just left her alone. I'd give him my

100

soul, devote my life to him... But all he said was, 'The time for deals is done for you have nothing left worth trading.'"

Q.

Patient #132117:

"He made me watch. Watch as he whispered in my voice and touched her with my hand though it no longer belonged to me...He goddamn defiled her. Fucked her like she was some machine. Pulled at her dress and made her suck his fingers before working them into her ass. Made her gag on my cock until she was coughing and her eyes were tearing from try-ing not to puke. I could tell she wasn't enjoying it much, but she loves me and would do anything if I asked her to... one of the reasons I married her...

"The pig gave me another one of his visions as he came inside her.

"It was some horrible pig-faced fetus growing and grow-ing until he was a pig-faced boy who drowned kids by the creek and skinned cats alive to hear them cry. And when he was a pig-faced man, he'd killed us all and went loose into the world and, Christ, doc... The things he did...The others he bred...

"And it was going to come from my wife. Would grow inside her. Eat her alive before he killed me and then all the ones who couldn't see his pig-face for what it was would be like lambs..."

Q.

Patient #132117:

"After the vision, he gave me back my body. His presence lingered there like someone a little too fat borrowed your coat, but I could move my hands and close my eyes.

"I wanted to hold her and tell her I was sorry for not being able to protect her, that I know none of it was her fault. But, she just smiled up at me, propped herself up on her elbows, and kissed me. '*Grosero*,' she said then went to make coffee.

"'What were you so furious about?' the pig said. 'That cunt seemed to like my way of fucking, huh? Maybe I taught her a few things.'"

Q.

Patient #132117:
    "Yes, that's when I followed her into the kitchen."

Q.

Patient #132117:
    "She was fiddling with the coffee maker in her robe."

Q.

Patient #132117:
    "I wasn't trying to kill her, understand? I had the knife, her back was turned. If I wanted her dead, she'd be dead."

Q.

Patient #132117:
    "I was trying to cut that thing out of her. That piglet of his. Sure, he used my nuts, but it was *his* seed. I couldn't let it grow. Not in my wife. Even if it didn't kill her out-right, the things to come would've. Being the mother of

something born out of our collective nightmares... Not for my wife.

"It had to come out... she won't understand it now, but she will someday. I can explain it to her. I know it hurt when I cut her, that I don't doubt. The blood must've scared her too... she'd always been real faint at the sight of blood... I knew where to get her, though. It would make sure the piglet wouldn't take, but wouldn't kill her."

Q.

Patient #132117:

"I guessed at where I had to cut her. It... there wasn't much thought going into it... just fear. I knew what was going to happen, knew what a piglet running around would mean for all of us... I just put the knife wherever it felt right..."

Q.

Patient #132117:

"How do you think she reacted? She screamed real loud, whacked me with the coffee pot, and ran out the door yelling for help."

Q.

Patient #132117:

"I wasn't following her. Not that time. After she left, I got the knife and went outside regardless of my burning face... I think it cleared me up.

"The burns.

"Kept me thinking straight. Reminded me that I needed to go gut that pig once and for all. But, when I got to the truck, he wasn't there."

Q.

Patient #132117:

"Doc, I've got to wonder if you're even listening to me if the question you came away with was, 'How did a pig get out of the truck?' That. Fucking. Pig. Is. A. Demon. If it can open a door into people's minds, why would a Dodge Dakota give him any trouble? Especially one with an open window.

"You know the rest: cops showed up. I didn't fight them. Now, I'm here."

Q.

Patient #132117:

"I know she's all right and healing up. If she were gone, I'd feel it in my heart... and he'd tell me. Be the first to know and I'd be the second."

Q.

Patient #132117:

"He tells me lots of things about all the people that I know. Shows me their depravity and wretchedness. Tells me their secrets. Things *they* don't even know."

Q.

Patient #132117:

"For one, I know she's pregnant. *He* told me that."

A Pig Named Orrenius

Q.

Patient #132117:

"If you have any sense, you'd cut that thing out of her and burn it to ashes."

Q.

Patient #132117:

"*His* son? Doc, he doesn't understand the concept. There's no such thing as a bond with that pig. Only contracts. Families are the meat that makes you stronger or kills you for the effort. That wouldn't be his son. Just a duplicate born of our world. Something subtler and more horrible than anything I've ever seen... And my wife's just the incubator. That's what we all are. Grow houses for things like that pig, god curse his name..."

—ETC.—

THE FISHER

The mosquitoes were hell that night. Even with the rain and the makeshift tent, Felipe found himself slapping at his dusty neck and itching wherever his flesh was exposed. He used his knife--an old bayonet blade set in a wooden handle tied with twine--to cut strips of jerky. The tent was little more than a dusty brown horse blanket draped over a low hanging willow branch, but Felipe knew he was lucky to have even that.

He'd fallen in with a small band of thieves from Cenizo in order to earn enough to make the trip to La Salle. Their stick-up at a small bank turned sour at the start when one bandit shot the old clerk in the jaw and gave the sheriff's mother, who was there only to change a dollar bill for the collection plate, a heart attack in the process.

The sheriff hunted the small band, hung two and shot the third in the leg so he could get close enough to stab the man to death personally.

Felipe escaped through the *monte* during the stabbing, keeping low until nightfall, where he walked by moonlight, the image of his fellow thieves twitching at the end of a noose fresh in his mind. For the first two days, Felipe dared not make a fire, dared not sleep for more than a few minutes or linger at a creek lest that sheriff be nearby on some ridge, rifle ready.

When he saw no pursuit, even on the days he wedged himself into some hole or gap in the broken landscape to look and listen for the approach of shod horses on the hills, he decided he needed to build a small fire of just a few twigs of mesquite. Something easy to smother if he had to hide.

The Fisher

A storm was in sight as he hunted for kindling and the drizzle, a mist that seemed to hang over everything, soon followed. He found the willow tree and threw his stolen blanket over a branch and decided to be cold and alive.

Felipe was so small a man that the horse blanket was enough to curl under, though it did little against the armada of mosquitoes. The mist around him made the brush a darker place than the previous nights. The sounds of night birds and coyotes were drowned out by the hissing of the rain. A sound did drift on the wind.

A voice, Felipe thought.

He laughed the notion away, knowing he was careful and many days out of Cenizo. The dark as well as the wild country played tricks on weary travelers. He stuck a piece of jerky out into the rain to loosen it a bit when he saw the flicker of something through the drooping shrub trees.

A flame, perhaps, Felipe thought, but the light was lost in the heavy mesquite and huisache branches.

He ate a few softened pieces of jerky, thinking to cover his hands and face completely to ward off the mosquitoes kicked up by the rain. But, the flash of fire came once more as did the faint voice.

At first, Felipe curled closer to the trunk of the willow tree, thinking the light was a lawman's torch or lantern. Yet, the more he watched it through the waterlogged leaves, the more the man knew it was no torch. It was constant and wide like a campfire.

Let them camp, he thought. *I'll stay here and suffer and leave tomorrow morning. See if they left scraps.*

Scraps. The thought of what the camp could be eating—tortillas and beans and hot coffee or stew and venison—stayed with Felipe as he chewed on his jerky. Felipe thought about all the possibilities, and it was the combination of imagining the travelers eating *pozole* and a mosquito biting his cheek that urged him forward.

Horse blanket over his head, Felipe made his way to the flames. He used the thick cloth to move aside a tangle of mesquite branches when the fire was only yards away. The thorny tree clung to his blanket and he wrestled with it, cursing the plant and all its kind. Then, the voice returned.

No longer was it faint and indecipherable. Now, it was a howl of agony. The frantic bleating of a woman in electrifying pain.

Felipe took the knife from his belt and ran toward the sound, toward the flames dancing beyond the thicket of brush. When he cleared the tree line, he fell back at the sight.

It was a bowl of blue fire. And in the center of the flames was a woman in the panicked throes of torture. Five ropes untouched by the flames held her by the neck and appendages. Even with her face twisted into a mask of suffering and the way her naked flesh shivered, Felipe knew her to be beautiful. He tried to crawl toward her, but the fury of the pyre had him fidgeting, the byproduct of instinct and desire at war.

She seemed to sense Felipe there. Her head shot sideward, digging the enchanted rope deeper under her jaw. Her eyes were both beautiful and pathetic. She shouted, "Help me! Please! By the saints, save me!"

Felipe couldn't move.

"Please!" the woman begged on her fiery bed. "A *bruja* bound me here! Her husband thought me pretty and she did *this* to me!"

Looking into her maddened eyes, Felipe stood.

"Cut the ropes!" she yelled. "Cut the ropes!"

Felipe shook himself from the shock of it and went for the nearest rope. It was of a thick make with what looked like the twisted pages of hymnals braided through it. His knife was dull and the handle gripped the blade poorly, making it an ordeal to cut the fibers. The rain and jitters didn't help either. His arms turned wooden and heavy with the first rope, his knife slipping with every cut. Her screams distorted time itself, making each futile pass of his blade stir up a greater panic in him. He freed her legs and was nearing the last rope on her arms when the blade came free of the handle.

He floundered on the ground for the blade, gritting his teeth against the sound of the woman, the beautiful woman whose only crime was grace, burning alive in some unholy fire. Felipe found the blade and set to cutting the rope furiously, uncaring of the knife digging into the heels of his palms.

The Fisher

The screams. The screams. All he could hear were the screams and the crackling of witchcraft.

With only her neck bound, Felipe tried to pull her out of the flames, but he doubted a team of bays could dislodge her. Felipe chopped at the taut rope with the piece of steel, sawed at it, and cut one of his thumbs to the bone in the race against the woman's hellish pain. With the bayonet blade pressed against bone, the final rope gave way, but still, she couldn't be moved.

Despite the flames, Felipe went to her, ready to fight through the fire. The earth swelled under his feet and on each side of Felipe, two giant eyes opened and focused on him. It was then that the woman went limp and rose into the air. The flaming figure's light revealed what creature Felipe had truly released. The flames swiveled from a massive toad's head and the light cast odd shadows against its rock-like skin.

The creature rose up as much as its front legs allowed, dwarfing Felipe.

The man fell back and tried to crawl away, but it was like trying to run from a living hill bearing down on him.

The creature reached out and pinned Felipe to the ground with his muddy foot. The weight of the arm alone pulverized the Felipe's legs. The force of its tongue rocketing at the man snapped his spine on impact and pulled the battered body into the creature's mouth. Once in its mouth, the fisher let the weight of Felipe's corpse do the work of sliding into its guts.

Finished, the fisher dimmed the humanoid beacon atop its lure and moved through the brush in search of other travelers in the night.

—ETC.—

THE RAPIST OF PERVERSION PARK

I.

Dos Santos Park sat at the corner of Davis and Healy in a small town of no more than a thousand--twelve hundred during Thanksgiving or Christmas. The park, during the day, boasted a pebble pit with a set of rusty swings and monkey bars that in the summer were hot enough to burn skin and a sturdy plastic slide decorated with the cave paintings of transients and teenagers, felt-tip homages to awkward sex and who got stuck in what hole by whom. By nightfall, the parking lot was full of cars of teenagers fucking and fondling and the nearby dugout was a hotspot of lost virginities and drug use. To most of Genoskwa, Texas, the corner of Davis and Healy was known as Perversion Park with good reason.

At night, it was *the* place to be besides the local burger joint, Stout's. Some kid always had a case of warm beer in the back of his daddy's pick-up and the smell of ditchweed was soon to fill the neighborhood around the park. But, Genoskwa was a small place where everyone judged, yet no one said anything on the record. They knew nothing for certain, but would often say things like 'I coulda sworn I saw the Perkins' boy smoking cigarettes out at Perversion Park. Was holding it funny, too, if I ain't mistaken' or 'I thought I saw Mr. Saldivar's sedan out at Perversion Park, but it couldn't've been. That girl of his is *too* good for that.' And it was one of those kind of discussions, the ones held in hushed tones, behind raised hands, that weighed heavily on the mayor's mind.

Mayor Guillermo Munguia sat in his office, shades drawn, face in his hands. At points, he felt himself slipping into an exhausted sleep. He fought the urge, knowing another nightmare would be waiting. The ones where he's campaigning at the town hall, the buntings and banners and streamers flapping in the smelly A/C. The whole town was there to hear him speak, Including, out of some boyhood fantasy, Ursula Endress in her Bond bikini, though his dream-version was elderly and withered. A spry General Custer was there too, though trapped in the body of a ten year old black boy.

The people clapped and he smiled. Waved. Spoke of values and safety and a future that wouldn't look like the rest of the state and beyond. *The world may be going down the toilet*, he'd say in a dreamy autotune, *but not my town. Not on my watch.* He'd hit the podium for emphasis, nodding along with his constituents. Even in his dream, he tried to count the number of registered votes there. All of them took his words as truth, a bold public declaration that he'd be a guide to keep the town from straying.

Then, the crying would start.

An infantile sob would pierce through the claps and whistles and J. P. Sousa marching music. Every time he had the dream, the people turned to regard some center point, the origin of the whining. They'd all step back in disgust, their cheers now whispers hidden behind hands, slowly revealing the cause of the commotion: Prudencia. His teenage daughter. His angel.

There she'd be, thrown in the center of the room, hair caked into dread-locks by her own aged vomit, shirt pulled up over her round belly and jean skirt rolled up enough to reveal her inside-out underwear. Eyes closed, she'd bleat and bleat until, even in his dream, Mayor Munguia thought he'd die of shame. It was at the height of his horror that Prudencia whined *Daddy... Daddy...* in the shrill voice she got when she was drunk or mad or during her woman's time. *I think I'm pregnant. It was a nice party, though...*

The room gasped and Mayor Munguia felt a dull, dreamy pain in his chest. A sensation hardly represented, but real enough to cause him to panic in his dream.

Don't worry, I've gotta list of suspects, she'd laugh while pulling out a wad of business cards. Here, a strong wind would catch the cards and send them flying, their crisp edges hissing in the air, until the room was covered in a dizzying plague of possible sperm donors. His ears would fill with the *thwap, thwap, thwap* of cards, all the boys he knew desecrated his daughter...

Always, the last thing the mayor heard before shooting up in bed was the *thwap, thwap, thwap* of the cards.

"This a bad time, Willie?" the mayor heard from his door. "Been knocking for like a minute." It was Sheriff Christopher Espen, a short man of forty whose thin-skinned face turned an almost permanent pink from years of living under the harsh Texas sun.

"Sorry, sorry," Mayor Munguia said, motioning the sheriff in. "Come in, please."

"You feeling all right? Look like you're coming down with something, if you ask me," Sheriff Espen said as he sat. He reached into his pocket for a pack of cigarettes and offered one to the mayor, who waved it away.

"No, no," he said. "I'm fine. It's just... didn't really get any sleep last night."

"Just part of getting older," the sheriff said.

"I wish I'd just die already," the mayor replied. His hands clamped the sides of his head as if keeping all the horrible thoughts from bursting out of his skull in a shower of gray and red. "I was waiting up for Pru. She didn't get home until four-something."

"Hell... she's just getting to that age," Espen said. "Nothing to worry about."

"The hour wasn't... the worst part of it, Chris," the mayor said, his hands coming together over his eyes. "I was sitting there on my chair, lamp off and all that... Imagine, sitting in the damn dark until four. Can't even tell you the kinds of crazy stuff I was getting ready to tell her. It was going to be *the* big one. The one that'd get her to stop running around this town, drunk and crass... Doesn't even have the decency to try to hide it. Sixteen years of living and not one ounce of shame in her. Can you imagine, Chris... kicked out of school for two weeks for giving it up under the god damn bleachers. Not with just one boy neither. No. One boy wouldn't suffice to give me a damn heart attack." The mayor shook his head and went to his bottom drawer, which held a small bottle of whiskey.

The mayor put the bottle on the table and let go of it for a second. He wore his worry and lack of sleep on his face, distorting his features into patches of unhealthy sagging. He eyed the bottle, nodded, and took it up.

"Jesus, Will, it's morning," Sheriff Espen said, making a move for the bottle.

"Only if you've slept," Mayor Munguia said before drinking from the bottle. "If you ask me, the sun just butted into my shitty, shitty night. Spent it pissed, my guts all hurting and my teeth clenched. Then, to top it off, I wouldn't even say that Pru even got home. More like she was delivered."

"Don't tell me--"

"Dropped at my doorstep. Whatever boy she's taken a liking too or just has a marijuana cigarette handy... whoever she was with just dropped her on my doorstep," Mayor Munguia said and took a sip from his bottle.

"Must've been rough, did she--"

"I froze," Munguia said, not meeting his friend's stare. "I opened the door, found her with the goddamn welcome-mat on her like a blanket. Then... all that stuff I thought of... all the things I was going to say to hurt her, to break her... Shit, it just went out the window. I folded. Make-up all smeared, basted in beer and pot smoke... Should've tossed a bucket of ice water on her, the old 'skillet alarm clock' like when we were young. *But*," the mayor sighed. "I just picked her up and got her on the couch and said all the ranting and raving could wait until tomorrow, though I couldn't even say I was mad anymore."

"Just a sign of a good dad," the sheriff said.

"This morning," the mayor said. He smiled. It was an expression of both confidence and acute desperation. "I was making coffee and she told me to, what was it... Oh, yeah. She told me to 'keep it the fuck down' then called me a dumb piece of shit. When I raised my voice to her, she gave me the finger and told me 'to tell it to one of the hicks that gives a flying fuck.'"

The sheriff opened his mouth a bit as if with some retort, but found nothing sufficient to say.

"I'm at my wit's end," the mayor said.

"Maybe you could get Reverend Gregg to talk to her," the sheriff offered. "Bet he can--"

"She's liable to get me and Iracema kicked right out of the parish," the mayor said. "And, I can't ask Iracema. *God*, to give birth to a girl you're terrified of… She acts like a wild dog's on the couch. Won't say a thing but 'please' and 'sorry' and nothing else."

"Can't stop them at that age," Espen said, thinking the words wise, though they too were insufficient.

"But, I *can* take that venue they love," the mayor said. "Force them away from that goddamn park. There's nothing but manure farms for twenty miles. They'll be forced back into the light of Genoskwa. Places where we can police easier."

"Not a one in this town'll let you take the park, Willie," Espen scoffed. "Barely let the last mayor get the tax hike to get it built."

"Of course I'm not proposing that, but, I was thinking that we could make it a more unattractive place," the mayor said, sipping his bottle. He motioned for a cigarette and lit it with a cheap lighter. The mayor puffed at it as though for the taste alone, letting the smoke fill his cheeks only to dribble out. "I don't know… we could scare them away, I guess. That might work."

"Like put on monster costumes and stuff?" Espen asked, chuckling.

"Good God, no! This isn't a cartoon," Munguia scoffed. "I thought we could make up some crime. A criminal that stalks that area. A killer, maybe."

"You want me to make up a murder?" Espen asked. "It's a small town. Everyone'll ask around until there's a head count. Knowing kids, they'll just think a couple of murders makes the park that much cooler."

"A rapist then," the mayor said. "No one wants to be raped… oh, no. If we want to get the word out, the paper would need the guy's name and--"

"We'll just say we can't disclose that because of the on-going investigation or some shit like that," the sheriff said.

"Yes, yes, yes," the mayor said. "It's the kind of thing no one talks about and no one dare ask about. We just need…" The mayor trailed off, his synapses firing off, the web of his scheme forming. The process was a slow one. "Do you think Rigby could get a sketch. Something generic. Hispanic. Between eighteen and twenty-eight. About 5'5 to 5'11."

"Hell, that sounds like most of the town," Espen said.

"Exactly," the mayor said, snapping his fingers. "It'll get the kids away from that park at night and it'll damn near give you free rein when it comes to hassling those kids."

"And what happens when everyone expects me to catch this nobody," the sheriff asked.

"He can be *anyone*," the mayor said. "He'll be a drifter for all you know. It'll be our Santa Claus. Don't keep in line, the Rapist'll get you. Stay out past curfew and *bam!* The Rapist is there, creeping out of the shadows. I swear, if we do this right, we can keep the next twenty years of kids in line. Our ace in the hole. Foolproof. Absolutely foolproof."

II.

There wasn't a place in Genoskwa that wasn't in view of the wanted posters. The quick sketch of an anybody under a baseball cap. As soon as the paper printed the article, the change Mayor Munguia hoped for started happening. The articles worked their magic on Genoskwa and teenagers--girls mostly--were locked indoors when the sun went down, which led to more teenagers--mostly boys--staying home as well.

There were rumors by the dozen. In those weeks, any child who missed a day of school was labeled a victim in whispers and any of the many men in town that fit the description called Sheriff Espen themselves to give alibis for the days in question.

Even Prudencia, his daughter, showed the effects of the fictional rapist. She no longer went out in the evenings, due mostly to her parents' new use of the rampant sex-offender as ammunition, and lounged around the house, tinny music coming from her oversized headphones They ate dinner together and had mildly forced conversations during which Prudencia reserved her sarcastic voice and thinly-veiled insults for the end of the meal.

The mayor had never slept better now that his daughter spent her nights in the room down the hall instead of the single-cab of some dusty Chevy.

And, the true beauty of his plan, of this Rapist of Perversion Park, was that it never stopped working. It could be used over and over. When the park was vandalized by a group of three boys, the paper reported that another assault had occurred and a tighter watch was kept by both sheriff and citizen. Calls would flood in from concerned citizens saying things like 'better get Espen over to the park. A bunch of kids are out there... liable to get raped, the fools' or 'I smell something funny in the air, bet that rapist is out there smoking drugs and waiting to pounce.'

Soon, the community took up a watch program that really put an end to any funny business at the park. Concerned fathers, rifles in hand, took turns patrolling the park in shifts, making Perversion Park a social spot of the past.

But, like all diseases, physical or social, when a treatment was found, the sickness adapted. One day, when the rapist had six 'victims' to his name, Prudencia came home before sundown red-eyed and reeking of pot. When Mayor Munguia tried to talk to her, he found his daughter unresponsive and giggling. The scolding ended with him tomato red and Prudencia pulling at the end of his moustache, her slurred voice going *qwerk! qwerk! qwerk!*

The next day, Iracema told him that Pru had been at Mark Duncan's house the day before.

"The founder of the Dos Santos Park Patrol?" Mayor Munguia said. "How could that--"

"She said all the patrol's kids are throwing parties," Iracema said. "She said 'if Duncan's dumb enough to announce to the world where they are all the time, why'd they expect any different?' Can you imagine, the kids of this town--our own daughter among them--taking something good like this and turning it into an excuse to party. I suppose it's safer indoors than it is out there with this god-awful rapist on the loose." She shivered. "Is Espen any closer to catching him?"

"Working on it, working on it," Munguia said, thinking of how to use his made-up man to his advantage. "He's clever, very clever," he told his wife. She started to tell him something, but he stopped listening.

———◆———

Within the next week, the Rapist of Perversion Park struck twice, once breaking into a home and assaulting a drunk boy who'd passed out in a friend's spare bedroom. Then, a few days later, he lured another victim with marijuana, which was laced with some drug or the other. The names, like all the others, had been withheld since the victims were still in high school, classmates or friends of Prudencia. No one dared ask and no one, by the town's logic, would dare admit it.

There was no more stink of ditchweed and corner store incense cones. No more parties thrown at patrolmen's homes since now the patrols went beyond the park, spoiling the misadventure of youth. They flushed them out of the brush and from behind abandoned buildings and dirt alleys that cut through whole neighborhoods. Even seeing one armed patrol pass his window, Mayor Munguia knew it was worth it.

The day before, he'd been eating dinner with his family and told the story of when he'd gone deep-sea fishing with Iracema on their honeymoon. Munguia snared a tuna and, after twenty minutes, managed to reel in the fish and snap a photo with his two prizes, the tuna and his new bride. Yet, moments after, the tuna floundered and sent Munguia tumbling into the sea. It was a poor, local charter boat from nearby that had no ladder and Munguia proved too big to lift, so they drove the boat with him holding onto a thin net. He told the table that he was just waiting for a shark to nibble at his toes, so most of the ride involved him urinating and then wondering if urine attracted sharks, which, in turn, made him urinate even more. As he told the story, a marvelous thing happened.

Prudencia laughed.

And it wasn't a vicious laugh, the kind that told the mayor his daughter thought him a fool or too stupid to see how ridiculous he was. No. It was a genuine laugh as though Pru had, without judgment, imagined her father and mother on their trip and could identify the comedy in his fall, in his irrational fear.

He stood in his office after dinner, the sound of the laugh in his mind, when the sheriff came into the room without knocking. "Willie, we've got us a *huge* problem," he said, his face pale. The radio on his belt was whispering and bleeping frantically. He turned it off. "Been non-stop. My radio is about to melt."

"How do you figure we've got a problem," Munguia said, turning and scooting his chair out to sit. "Seems to me things have been going great this month. I'd say--"

"They caught him," Espen said.

"Who? Wait... who caught who?" Munguia asked.

"They caught the Rapist."

III.

Mayor Munguia rode in the passenger seat of the sheriff's cruiser in silence. All he kept thinking of was the extent of what he was rocketing towards. He told himself that the people of Genoskwa were level-headed. No doubt they were currently scaring the hell out of a traveler by locking him in the filling-station bathroom or were huddled in the corner of Stout's suspiciously eying some trucker. But, he thought too of the hundreds of flyers, the days spent sketching out details with Espen to call into the paper, and his intestines felt like they wriggled into a square-knot. Mayor Munguia gripped his cramping belly and hoped nobody had been killed.

The sheriff, on the other hand, was panicked. Lights on, he blasted through the old downtown block and blew past the highway intersection. When he wasn't chanting 'oh-shit-oh-shit-oh-shit,' Espen was on the radio, trying to get some kind of information other than that a patrol had cornered the Rapist at Perversion Park.

He kept the windows down to listen for gunfire.

Turning the corner, neither man could see the park through the mob that crowded the corner of Davis and Healy. The sound coming from the gathered citizens of Genoskwa was a gale of jumbled words and curses. The red and blue lights did little other than cause a wave-like bucking that surged through the people. Even from the angle of the low cruiser, they counted a number of rifles and pistols clutched in upraised fists.

Once they exited the cruiser, there was a palpable lust for blood in the air. It caused another spasm to tighten Mayor Munguia's guts. The sheriff flipped a switch on the console in the cruiser and took the radio receiver in his hand. "All right, all right, folks," he said; his pose—half standing in and out of the cruiser with his arm propped on the door—made him seem calm, but the man's head looked scaly with sweat. "Disperse, disperse," he said, honking the horn.

At first, those closest to the cruiser turned and glared at him with such malice that he contemplated reaching for his pistol. The sheriff didn't know if it was the lights or the sight of the mayor and himself standing there, but the feral looks of friends and neighbors soon subsided. The looks faded into a general recognition. First, the crowd remembered Mayor Munguia and Sheriff Espen were men they knew. Second, the people recalled that the mayor and sheriff were men of authority for some reason they didn't immediately remember.

The people--teachers and bankers and waitresses and mechanics and war vets in their chairs--eventually parted, giving way to a sight that nearly made Mayor Munguia soil himself in horror.

Tied to the monkey bars by rope and belts knotted around his wrists was a man in his early twenties. Average on all accounts save the color of his skin, which was a mystery hidden under a coat of blood that sprung from his mouth and nose and cuts hidden in his hair. Two men were pulling at his ankles, the bindings making him go diagonal while two women armed with rocks beat the man's ribs and shoulders.

The mayor was certain the man was dead, but, as he approached, the poor soul spat a mouthful of blood and pled with them in what sounded like Spanish. Broken teeth and swollen lips made it gibberish. He faced them but he could no longer see, his eyes bloated and purple.

A man moved to strike him, but a general whisper of the mayor's arrival brought enough sense to him that he lowered his fist. At first, against the setting sun, his face twisted in rage, the man was nearly unrecognizable to the mayor. But the more civility that came to the man, the more he came to resemble Mark Duncan once more.

For a moment, the mayor was at a loss for something to say. "Let's... uh... Let's all just calm down," he finally said. He stood in front of the restrained man, his fiction made real, and put his hands out like the practiced orator he was. "Why doesn't someone tell me and the sheriff there exactly what's going on."

Like one fool with a hundred voices, the crowd bellowed accusations.

"One at a time, people!" the mayor called out, patting the air to silence them.

Mark Duncan was the first to speak. "We caught him peeping into May Sue Jensen's bedroom window," he said, each word reigniting the righteous anger burning below the surface. "One of the patrols tried to question him--"

"That's my job, Mark," Sheriff Espen said, joining the men and wincing at the sight of the supposed rapist.

"*My* job as a *man* is to protect me and mine from some no-good, raping piece of shit," Duncan snarled, the anger twisting his face again. "He ran too. Ran like hell until we caught him. Put that sketch in the paper right up next to his face. Matched to the word."

The mayor and sheriff exchanged looks.

"Maybe so, Mark," the sheriff said. "But, we've got procedures. You can't just go around tying people up--"

"That ain't no *person*," Duncan spat. "According to *you*, he's gone at eight of our kids *that we know of.* God knows how long this bastard's been eyeing our town. Lusting and scheming with his dick in his hand."

"Even if that's the case, Mark, this ain't the Wild West," the sheriff said. "You should've--"

"What?" Duncan roared. "Let him get away? Let him go off and rape again?"

All around them, the more rational members of the crowd started thinking, but the ones still whipped up by the smell of blood and retribution wanted to see justice served. As the two men argued, the crowd called for Mayor Munguia's opinion. He was the elected leader of the town and it should be by his word that the notorious Rapist of Perversion Park be dealt with there or by the courts.

With the eyes of the entire town on him, Mayor Munguia retreated into his happy-place: there were no people there for it was his kitchen tucked safely away in the past where it held his beautiful Iracema and his newly returned Prudencia, who had laughed like she had when she was a little girl and used to chase dragonflies out in the yard, content with the little universe that was the Munguia's home, their family. It was all she needed, for her father was her hero for nothing more than existing and her mother the most beautiful woman to walk the earth because hers was the last face her little girl saw at night. It was a beautiful blanket memory that the crowd would not let him keep.

"I... uh... now, uh... we've...," he stammered. The mayor knew there was no way he could tell them to arrest the poor soul tied to the monkey bars. There'd be a trial. Witnesses would need to be called and for that, records and documents and witness statements would be demanded. Rape kits catalogued and their findings faxed to attorneys and a judge. The truth would come out before that when the man, once restored and mended enough to speak, was questioned about a series of rapes that never happened. But, there was no way the mayor could tell them then and there. They'd kill *him*. To hear their mayor lied about such a thing so he could keep a tighter leash on his daughter, so she could laugh at the table again, as angry as they were... they'd only get angrier.

Mayor Munguia focused on the bleeding man splayed out like a gutted buck. Mark Duncan looked at him and the sheriff too, the former eager for an order and the latter for an exit. When the mayor opened his mouth to speak, he remembered the notes of his daughter's laugh. He amplified the sweetness of it so that the memory droned out the sound of his words so that all he saw was his family, happy and safe. He could no longer see the lusty crowd throwing up their hands, shouts rumbling through even the air in his lungs.

One of the crowd cut the man's bindings.

The sheriff watched silently.

Not far from the playground, someone threw a rope over the thick branch of an oak tree.

—ETC.—

Sign on the Dotted Line

M rs. Mullens sat on a long bench bolted to the hospital wall. The ward was long and smelled of disinfectant tinged with the stale scent of bedpans left full. Her shoe clacked woodpecker-like on the linoleum floor and she adjusted her glasses for the third time since she'd sat down. The twins, Ed Jr. and Edwina May, sat on both ends of her, kicking their legs off the edges of their seats. Edwina May called for her mother.

"Hush now, Eddie May," Mrs. Mullens hissed at her. "I don't know when the doctor's coming any more than you do. But, I'm sure your daddy will be just fine."

"But, he got bit by a rattler," the girl countered.

"I read that rattlesnake venom can kill a man in an hour," her brother grumbled. "Even less if he panics. Hear that, Sis? You having to put on your day shoes might've killed Daddy."

"Shut up!"

"The both of you be quiet!" Mrs. Mullens yelled. "Don't make me scream in this hospital. And, Ed Jr., your father wasn't bit. The snake just nicked him. It barely broke the skin."

"Daddy was screaming like it was more than just that," Edwina May said.

"That's because your father is a big baby," Mrs. Mullens said. She perked when the double-doors at the end of the hall swung open, but only a nurse came out. Her leg shaking resumed. Flustered, she opened her purse and took out a stick of spearmint gum, which drew her children's hands like a magnet. She fished out two more pieces and handed them to the twins.

"I'm hungry, Momma," Edwina May said after a moment.

"I swear, Eddie May, I'll take you out into that parking lot. Don't think I won't either."

The double doors opened and the hard clack of the doctor's snake-skin boots bounced off the walls. Dr. Ramos was a tall bald man with a pregnant belly solidly protruding from his torso. As he walked down the hall, he adjusted the long cigarette behind his ear. He looked up at the family and grinned warmly in a fluid, practiced motion. "Mrs. Mullens," he said, tipping his imaginary hat to her.

"Is he--"

"He's just fine," he assured her.

She sank back into the bench and sighed. "Oh... Dr. Ramos... thank you so much. Oh, what a relief."

"See," Edwina May told her brother. "I didn't kill daddy."

"Yet," the boy snarled.

"The both of you, hush," Mrs. Mullens seethed.

"Mrs. Mullens, there were some complications," Dr. Ramos said frankly. Before she could stammer her questions, he called a nurse from the station. "Nurse Serrato, why don't you take these two for a little something to eat." He took a ten dollar bill and gave it to her. "Go on now, kids. You wouldn't think it, but they make a mean cheeseburger in the cafeteria."

Once the twins were out of sight, Dr. Ramos took a seat beside Mrs. Mullens and the cigarette from his ear. He tapped the filter against his clipboard and let out a long sigh. "Mrs. Mullens, I don't know how to say this, but... there was a bit of a mix-up with the paperwork."

"What kind of mix-up?"

"Well, it seems that you accidentally wrote that your husband could be given penicillin. It wasn't until we actually administered it to him that we saw the allergic reaction," Dr. Ramos continued.

"Oh, God," Mrs. Mullens gasped. "What kind of reaction? He's not going to--"

"No, no," Dr. Ramos told her. "Normally, there is some localized swelling, but, in your husband's case...well, his testicles swelled to the size of oranges. And not collectively, but both. We had to remove them."

"That means... Ed'll not have his--"

"For the moment," Dr. Ramos told her. "Mrs. Mullens, didn't your husband tell you about our facility? About the Clinic?"

"No," she replied. "He just said this was the only place that would take his insurance."

Dr. Ramos slid the cigarette behind his ear and whistled softly. "Mrs. Mullens," he said. "Here at this branch of the Clinic, we offer a number of unorthodox services. Services you're your husband took part of many years ago. Now, these services can be very helpful in these kinds of situations. You see we can transplant a new set of testicles onto your husband. We've been housing a replicate of him for a number of years. Fifteen by my count."

Mrs. Mullens didn't respond.

"To put it bluntly, a clone. He's housed it here for exactly such a medical emergency. Within the week, we'll have the transfer done. And, with another week for observation, we'll release your husband back to your care."

"That's wonderful!" she gasped. "But, he never told me about his replicate."

"I wouldn't be surprised," Dr. Ramos said, nodding. "The use of replicates is frowned upon in religious communities such as ours. They're fairly popular in larger cities and most other countries, but it seems Texas wants to hold out due to the evangelical ramifications. There is one issue with your husband, though."

"What's that?"

"Here at the Clinic, we're only able to house healthy and, frankly, complete replicates."

"So, what does that mean?"

"Two things, really," the doctor said. "You can either leave it to us and we'll euthanize the replicate."

"How horrible!"

"Or, we can release it into your care."

Mrs. Mullens stood up and trembled as if her words fought to be out of her throat. "If that thing'll make my husband whole again... then you just give it to me. Euthanize... I know what that means around here. No, sir. You won't put Doctor .45 to it. Give it on over to me."

"It's all the same to us, Mrs. Mullens," Dr. Ramos said, flipping his clipboard around. "Go ahead and sign on the dotted line then."

———◆———

Ed Mullens returned home with a cane. With each step, his thighs jostled his newly implanted testicles, sending a hot wave of nausea up into the pit of his stomach. But, even with pain at every step, he seemed livelier, bolder. He woke late, enjoying the excuse of recovery to stay in bed longer.

The replicate, Chubbs as the children called it, adjusted as well as it could. The Clinic's care had left it devoid of speech and manners. Mrs. Mullens soon treated it with the same love she would a cat or dog. She used encouraging tones, though it could not understand her. For a week, Chubbs could not eat at the table, attacking its food violently as though used to the dry foods doled out to cattle and goats. But, with the help of a spray bottle and a pocketful of hard candy, Mrs. Mullens was able to teach it to eat quietly.

"Eddie May," she said at dinner. Outside, there was the loud report of a shotgun.

"Yes, momma," the girl said.

"What'd he say?" Mrs. Mullens asked her daughter.

"He said he'd be in in a minute."

The shotgun went off and the deep baritone of Ed's voice laughed and hooted.

"What's he doing out there?" Ed Jr. asked.

Mrs. Mullens scooted out her chair, which startled Chubbs, and she scratched behind his ear to calm him. "You all go ahead and eat. I'll get him. Make sure Chubbs eats and don't none of you go torturing him neither. If it wasn't for him, God only knows what your daddy would be like."

"Yes, ma'am," the twins grumbled.

Mrs. Mullens went out into the fresh air. It was thick with the powdery fragrance of huisache. The evening chill was setting in and she closed her sweater around her. She found him leaning on an old ash tree, sipping a beer. His shotgun laid broken in the crook of his arm. He reloaded it.

"Hun, ain't you coming in for some supper?" she asked him.

"Naw, Maureen," he said with a grin. In the dusk made the creases around his eyes show deeply. His eyes were two green pools surrounded by cracked skin. Yet, the look he shot her was one she seldom saw. It was the look of playful mischief. "I'm going to stay out here a bit," he chuckled. "I'm almost done with the shells I picked up today."

"Shells?" she asked, noticing the pile around the tree. Red tubes blackened and torn at the ends laid like dead wasps in the soft dirt. There were at least fifty. "What are you shooting at anyway?" she asked slowly before letting her eyes drift. The thick clumps of cacti looked like an enormous mandible of broken teeth. The cast shadows were polka-dotted with holes of light The smell of pulpy chloroform hung sweet in the air, but it only made her tense. "What the hell did you do, Ed?"

"What?"

"I said, what the hell did you do?"

"I'm just having a little target practice. Plus, those paper targets they sell ain't worth a shit for a shotgun. I'd have to staple one in after every shot. Matching the boxes, that'd be sixty. Not to mention the box of staples and the pallet."

"How much did the shells cost? I know they weren't the ones you had lying around."

"What's it matter?"

"We've got bills, Ed. That's what matters. You're out here shooting away thirty dollars," she huffed, waving her hand. "We've still got your bills from the Clinic. And don't forget Chubbs. He's got to eat same as us."

"I'll take care of it, then," he said, closing the gun in his hands.

"Don't you even joke like that, Ed," she barked. "If it wasn't for Chubbs, you'd be just like our old dog. Nutless. So, you show Chubbs some respect. I know you're enjoying what he gave you."

Ed aimed the shotgun off into the thicket of cacti and fired. A thick plate burst into a shower of pulp and thorns as the whole plant shook at the base.

"Maureen, not to fight with you, but Chubbs wouldn't have had anything to give me if it wasn't for me," he said, moving a fresh beer in a circle, to show the cycle of life that began and ended with him. "Shit, that's why I had the damn thing made in the first place."

He popped the cap off his beer and took deep gulps of it. "Hey, I agree with you about his... uh, gift. I feel like a new man," he said and leered at her. "Maureen, how 'bout you and me go behind this tree and do what we did on our third date? You know, the one at the carnival."

"*Ed*," she gasped, but the look in his eyes was enough to have her looking over her shoulder to the house. "Well... the twins'll take care of Chubbs," she said.

He circled the tree and said, "C'mon, honey."

"Fine," she giggled. "But you better be fast."

"No promises," he told her as he undid his pants.

Mrs. Mullens took one more look at the ranch house and pulled her shirt up so the dirt would not stain her clothes.

———————◆———————

"He wasn't always like this, you know," she told Chubbs. "Nope. Edward was one dependable man. I really just don't know what got into him." It was late and the house was quiet, the twins having been in bed for hours.

Chubbs made the broken figurines jauntily come together. The sound of a wet explosion stuttered out of his lips once they collided and he separated them with great sweeps of his flabby arms.

"He always said family came first," she sighed. "Look there, Chubbs," she told the replicate, pointing at a picture on the wall. Her painted fingernails drew his eyes but went no further. "That's Edward's great grandfather. He was half-Mexican and rode with Pancho Villa. I always hated that. But, if it wasn't for him, none of us would be here. Not Edward. Not you. Certainly, not me."

She withdrew her hand. Chubbs followed it with his eyes and batted at it.

"God help it, I still love that man," she blurted. "Always have. We've been sweethearts all our lives, you know. Well... on again, off again mostly. I'll never forget him leaving me for that grasshopper, Nora. One fight and he went a-runnin' to her. She wasn't all that pretty, just a big whore in a tight bra and short skirt." She looked down at Chubbs and grinned. "I know you're a copy of him, but I can't get over how much you look like he used to, Chubbs. Well, only chubbier. But, the doctor said that would happen to you on account of the procedure. Oh, Ed would kill me if he heard me brining up Nora, though. He tells me he's been making it up to me for my whole life and I know it. Just doesn't feel like it these days."

Chubbs rubbed his cheek against her leg and she pat his head. Hearing the crunch of gravel, she looked up through the kitchen window to the swing of headlights. The loose stones ground as the car went into a sudden halt. The parking brake was pulled. A cuss-filled cough. The boots clicked on the cement footpath. On the other side of the front door, keys fell and jingled. Ed came in fighting back a cough with a beer bottle in his hand. He kicked one boot off and struggled with the other.

"Where were you?" she asked him.

"Sweet shit!" he hissed and fell back onto the wall, shaking the pictures of first holy communions and weddings and cattle. "Maureen, you scared the hell out of me. What are you doing sitting here in the shadows like a damn assassin?"

"I was waiting for you to come home," she told him.

"Why?"

"*Why?*" she snipped. "Because," she said in a lower tone, "my husband of thirteen years was out until two something in the morning. Where the hell were you, anyway? You said you went up to Carl's to help fix his truck."

"I did," Ed agreed.

"What was wrong with it that it took you eight hours to fix it? Explain *that* to your wife."

"Don't be pulling that shit on me, Maureen," he said, putting down the bottle. "Well, I was there fixing Carl's truck, but I couldn't figure something out about it. It's one of those Asian models. So, we called up Gene and he got it figured out pretty quick--"

"How does that take eight hours, Ed?"

He shook his head at her in disbelief. "Maureen, will you let me finish? I'm getting to that. Well, Carl didn't have any money to speak of, so he decided to pay us in trade. He said this guy over at the XTC--"

"What the hell is the ecstasy?"

"No, honey. X.T.C. Just the letters."

"Well, what is it?"

"It's a gentleman's club," he said, letting his eyes drift over Chubbs. He winced and looked back to Mrs. Mullens.

"You left me here with the twins and Chubbs," she snarled. "You left us for eight hours, not to go back to work--that, I'd be happy to put up with--but for a house of ill repute?"

"It's not a damn bordello," he spat. "Carl just figured he'd get me and Gene drunk for all the help we gave him. All I did was have a few beers and bullshit with the boys."

"I'll bet," Mrs. Mullens said through a scowl.

"I'm being honest, Maureen," he said. "That's all I did."

"Oh, I'm sure. I'm sure you didn't even take one itty bitty peek at those naked girls"

"Now a man can't look?"

"A man can," she barked. "But not my husband. What's the matter with you? You never used to look before."

"I sure did, Maureen. I just kept my mouth shut about it."

Mrs. Mullens was struck silent. On the television, Herman Munster laughed his horsey laugh and Chubbs joined him. "Ed, if you're well enough to go spend all night at some cat house--"

"Christ…"

"Don't you take the Lord's name in vain in this house!" she yipped. "If you can do that, I think you can go back to work next week."

Chubbs nuzzled nervously against the hem of her skirt, making frightened blubberings once her hand reflexively went to his head and shoulders. Ed watched them in the white television glow that cast their shadows oddly against the wall's many picture frames.

"Aren't you going to say anything?" she asked.

"Yeah," Ed said. "Stop petting that thing like it was a damn cat. Just looking at the thing is gross enough, let alone my wife crawling into bed after playing with the damn thing." He picked up his beer and went down the hall. The bedroom door shut loudly.

She sat sipping warm tea from a white china cup. The housework was done. Everything save one room was dusted and swept. All the windows save one room were cleaned. Ed's room. Their room. Chubbs sat in the living room alone, the tool belt filled with cleaners and brushes still around his waist. With just the promise of a hard candy, Mrs. Mullens had trained him to follow her about like a walking shelf to assist her in her work. He'd even managed to be silent enough that Ed didn't stir. It was a little past noon. Ed was still asleep. Even a month after the surgery, he wasn't getting any better. Sure, everything worked, but now Ed slept all day and was out all night drinking. He'd come home and make a mess, grope her, and sleep until the afternoon again.

She stood over the sink to clean her cup when Ed appeared in the kitchen. His hair stood up and his skin carried the marks of his pillow. He wore nothing apart for his briefs and the web-like scars of his surgery. He tipped a carton of orange juice to his lips and drank heavy gulps with his red-eyes shut to the fluorescent light on the ceiling. He held the door open until he was finished and roughly put the empty sounding carton into the refrigerator.

"Honey," she said, drying her cup.

"Yeah," he said, rifling through the cupboards.

"Mr. Neilson called again," she sighed.

"Oh, yeah. What'd that old son of a bitch want?"

"He wanted to know if you were going to be back to work this week," she told him. She turned around and leaned against the counter, placing her hands on it in the posture of a hesitant bungee jumper.

"What'd you tell 'im?"

"That you'd call him. I told him you seemed well enough, though," she admitted.

He scowled. "What the hell did you go and tell him that for? Now he's thinking I'm just lazy." He slammed the cupboard door and groaned, rubbing his unshaven face slowly. "Well, I'm not calling him. I told him I'd be back when I felt good and ready."

"It's been a month, Ed," she told him flatly.

"Don't start with me," he warned.

"You started it with me, damn it! All you've been doin' is drinking and going round town with your stupid friends. You have a great time while I'm here cooking and cleaning. Taking care of our kids and Chubbs."

"The thing helps you, doesn't it?" Ed dared say.

"Yes, the *boy* takes five minutes out of my routine," she replied. "Sure, he holds the cleaner and keeps me company, but he doesn't pay the bills. You used to do that."

"Then whose money we using then, if not mine," Ed spat.

"That money is drying up fast, Ed. You think we can take another month of you going out all night drinking and whoring? You can't burn the candle at both ends," she snapped.

"I hate that damn job," he grumbled.

"Well, you can't very well go and get another one, can you? What else would you have us do?"

"You could start working again."

The very notion made her straighten and her eyes flutter as though his words were a pungent scent. "Ed, I haven't worked in ten years and even then, it was at the Piggly Wiggly bagging groceries. You want me to go and earn less than a dishwasher to support the five of us?"

"Five?"

"Chubbs is a person!"

"Says you," he said before walking away. He came back into the room, his wife in the same position, awaiting his response. He was wearing the clothes from the night before, a long-sleeved shirt with smudges of rouge around the cuffs and a pair of faded khaki's spotted with grease.

"Where do you think you're going?"

"Gene's place," he told her.

"Ed, I'm warning you," she said, pointing a finger at him. "Don't you walk out that door."

"Or what?"

"I don't know, but God help me, you'll know it once it's there."

"Can't wait," he retorted on his way out the door.

In the living room, Chubbs turned to the sound, halting his figurines in mid-flight. After a moment of stillness, he brought them together with his pudgy hands.

Mrs. Mullens wept into a lemony-scented dishrag.

<hr />

She sat alone in the car with the engine idle, waiting for the kids to cross the open lawn to their school. Mrs. Mullens lifted one hand to adjust her glasses and waved at the children's backs. She shifted the old paneled wagon out of the spot and rumbled onto the busy street. Sun-dried bottles clinked with every turn she made. The whole interior smelled of dried sweat and cheap cigars.

She pulled into an empty self-service car wash and parked alongside a blue trash bin. The backseat was first. Whiskey and beer bottles stood out like surfaced submarines among the crushed cans and greasy food wrappers. Two to a hand, Mrs. Mullens removed the bottles and tossed them in the bin, wincing when the glass clanked. The next batch she threw harder, but they would not break. She took the final bottle, a heavy tequila bottle of thick glass, and threw it like an axe.

Missile-like, the bottle shot into the bin, passing through the beer and whiskey pile, shattering them almost noiselessly until thudding heavily at the bottom of the bin.

She smiled.

She swept the cans into a pile with slow sweeps of her arm, frowning at the dozen cigarette burns black and acne-like in their randomness on the seats. The cans clattered hollow in the shards. She unfolded a tissue from her purse and collected the food wrappers one by one to dispose of. Under the seats, she found thirty cents of loose change and a lighter with a picture of a naked woman on the back. Snarling, she turned threw it into the bin, glad that the horrid thing was surrounded by trash. She felt further under the seats and tugged at a stretchy wrapper. The thing was caught on something and didn't pry loose until she got a good grip on it.

Once free, the torn thing slapped against her wrist.

She stared at it in confusion. A latex glove finger, yellow and dried, swaying like a flaccid sock in the slick breeze. Under the lens of her glasses, bits of dirt and single pubic hair caught her notice. Screaming, she threw the condom into the parking lot and trembled. Laying in the sun, the condom's open mouth stared at her lewdly, whispering to her, planting seeds.

The vomit came out of her violently, doubling her over and splashing against the ground.

Propping herself up on the car, she caught her breath and looked out to the streets. Cars passed her as if nothing had changed at all.

"I should go see Dr. Ramos," she huffed to herself. After a moment, she nodded to herself and got into the car.

———◆———

That night, she sat on the small armchair looking down at Ed, belly down on the bed, still in his clothes. One by one, she pulled the blankets off him, careful not to disturb him. With each spitty breath, the smell of cheap tequila drifted to her nose. Once he was uncovered, she folded the blankets and set them on her chair. She went into the bathroom and took the pre-threaded needle and spool from under the sink.

Before she began, she watched him and remembered. The way he was. The way he used to be. Without thinking, she reached out to stroke his disheveled hair. At the touch, he grumbled and slapped her hand away. "Not now, Nora," he sighed while adjusting himself. It took all of her not to dig the needle into his closed eye.

Mrs. Mullens started stitching him onto the bed at the ankles, pushing the needle through the dusty denim into their matrimonial bed and out again. The stitches were tight and erratic, some close to the boundaries of his clothes while others extended out. She was careful at the hem of his shirt, but made sure the stitches were tight. She went to the other side, kneeling on the bed and starting at his leg again. The whole process took her a meticulous hour of Ed groaning other women's names. They sounded like cheap drinks: Coco, Honey Drop, Daiquiri. She wondered which one he'd slept with in their car.

She went and replaced the needle and thread in the bathroom and looked around. A plunger was all she could find. She put her bare foot on the puckered rubber and pulled the wooden handle out roughly. She swung it at the empty air and tested its weight against her hand. With the impromptu cudgel in hand, Mrs. Mullens went into the room and fished a document out of the drawer. She slid it onto the nightstand, then placed a pen beside it. After giving the room a once over, she turned on the lights.

Ed groaned and tried to hide his face.

"Wake up, Ed," she whispered.

He cussed at her.

Tight-lipped, she went to his foot and snatched a sock off it. She crawled up to his face and forced the sock into his mouth. His eyes shot open and he struggled to free himself. Some of the threads popped, but in his drunkenness, he was helpless. Flopping like a fish, he cussed into the sock with his eyes altering from narrow slits to saucers. "Who was she, you son of a bitch? Who?" she seethed, barely above a whisper. "Who were you fucking around with?"

She hit him on the shoulder with the plunger handle. Then his thigh.

He howled and she tossed a pillow over his face and hit him again. She tore the pillow away and put the plunger handle to his cheek. "I found the condom, you bastard. Two months with a new set of balls and you cheat on me!" The handle clacked across the back of his skull and he went wild. Like a lizard turned over, he shook in his clothes, biting the spit-soaked sock. "You'd do that to our kids, Ed! You'd do that to us? I've been good to you, you lousy ingrate!"

She hit him across the back several times. Thwak. Thwak. Thwak.

"Now, you listen to me, Ed. You listening good?"

He nodded frantically.

"You want me to stop?" she spat. She hit him in the kidneys, going from one side of his torso to the other again and again.

He squealed and squirmed, his hands opening and closing as if electrified.

"You want me to stop, Ed?"

Tears puddled to the edges of his eyes.

She took the papers off the nightstand and showed them to him. "You see these? You want me to stop, you son of a bitch, then you sign on the dotted line."

He looked at her in confusion as if trying to decipher its purpose through his bleary eyes.

"Don't read it, Ed," she warned. She put the pages beside his hand and slid a pen into his shivering fingers. She clicked the pen open and positioned his hand. "Sign it," she told him with a thwak.

He scribbled his signature and she snatched it away, reading it. Satisfied, she threw him a look and sat at the edge of the bed. "You know what that was, Ed?"

He did not.

"It's a power of attorney agreement. As of right now, I own you. I own all the acres. The house. The car. Chubbs. And you. If I wanted to toss you in the tank and drown your sorry ass, I could because I own you."

His eyes narrowed. He breathed in gulps.

"Don't give me that look," she said, emphasizing her words with a strike at his elbow. "Let me tell you what you're going to be giving. That new brass pair. First thing in the morning, I'm taking you over to Dr. Ramos and you're getting them removed. I'm giving them right back where they came from. I don't care what it costs."

Ed shouted into the sock and thrashed.

Mrs. Mullens rose. "It ain't a question, Ed. I'll come and cut you loose in the morning." She went to the door and shut off the lights. "And if you wriggle free, don't think of coming out here and doing something to me. I thought of that. You're always calling him a dummy, but Chubbs can learn. So, just you try and come out and see what happens to you," she said and closed the door.

In the darkness beyond the door, Chubbs giggled to himself, standing erect like a soldier in formation, shotgun ready at his shoulder.

———•———

Mrs. Mullens sat with a cup of tea in her hands. She watched the bright afternoon sunbeams illuminating a few stubborn motes that resided in the house. The phone rang, but she did not move. From the other room, Chubbs went to the phone and answered it with an idiot's bark. He listened and brought the phone to Mrs. Mullens.

"Yes?" she said.

"Hey, honey," Ed answered. "I was just wondering, you want me to pick us up something to eat in town or are you cooking?"

"You just get us something," she said after a moment.

"Sounds good."

"How are you adjusting at work?" she asked.

"Fine, fine. I ain't on the line anymore, though, on account of getting too fat."

"Well, the doctor said that'll stop soon."

"I know," he replied. "I'll see you at home."

"Bye, Ed," Mrs. Mullens told him. She handed the phone to Chubbs, who put it on the receiver. "Come here, Chubbs," she said, patting the ground by her feet. Obediently, the replicate walked to her and sat. She pet his head, scratched his ears. "I wonder how you're holding up, nice and whole again," she said to him, grinning. Chubbs looked up at her. Her hand stopped and they sat frozen. There was something in his eyes that had her giggling like a teenager.

—ETC.—

MANOPLAS DE DIOS PLAY THE HORNED TOAD

For all of Sal's kids

I.

Apart, they were three teens pierced and tattooed, wearing tattered clothes safety-pinned together. They were walking targets in the small town of San Casimiro, Texas. Together, they were *Manoplas de Dios*, the only punk band worth a shit in three counties. They were all in Daryl 'Thrash' Offenbach's garage, filling their singer's home with brutal drums, discordant riffs, and a heavy baseline. Thrash barked the words of their song "Two Minutes of Hate" into an old microphone, which turned from a scratchy sound to that of feedback. He turned to see Rob 'Grosero' Velazco's face poised to sneeze, sending him too close to the amplifier. "All right, all right," Thrash spat. "Cut it," he told them, running his finger across his throat.

Thrash shook his head at Grosero, a lanky boy of seventeen with a shaggy mop of green hair. He let his bass dangle as he sneezed into his hands, which he wiped on his smelly ripped jeans. "Rob, seriously, take some fucking medicine," Thrash told him. "I feel your snot on the back of my neck in the middle of every song."

"Yeah right," Grosero told him. "You think the government allows medicine that actually cures anything? Hell no. All those big drug companies--your DuPonts and Pfizers and shit--are all subsidiaries to congressmen and senators. All it does is make me *think* I'm cured until my cold comes back, and I need more of that over-the-counter placebo shit at twenty bucks a dose."

137

"Maybe you get sick because you keep wiping snot all over your clothes," Rafa 'Travieso' Pizano said from behind the drums.

"Or do I get sick from all the chemicals pumped into our food?" Grosero offered. "In Brazil, they're finding bodies that won't rot on account of all the junk injected into the meat."

"All I know is I can see a turkey sandwich crusted to the back of your knees," Travieso said. "And Daryl's right, you need to take something. All your coughing and sneezing was what ruined the show in Gaston. A couple of those hippy gals would've let us run a train on them, but you had to go and cough on them during 'Virus Cake' and they went running."

"Don't blame *Gaston* on me," Grosero said before sneezing. "Head cold or not, I could've told you Gaston was going to be a disaster. Plus, those girls wouldn't've let you so much as touch them, let alone run a train on them."

In truth, Gaston had been a disaster.

Three weeks prior, old Cornelius Luca got drunk and drove to San Casimiro looking for his small home, which was back in Gaston. With the road tilting and shaking from drink, Luca parked his car a block from the Offenbach's red brick home. At first, Luca thought the sound of music was coming from his bloated stomach, but, after realizing he hadn't accidentally eaten a radio, he got out of the car and followed the sounds. *Manoplas de Dios* was halfway through "Biodegradable Education" before they noticed Luca jerking around like a dead man trying to dance. Despite Grosero's coughs, which ruined the song, Luca clapped and whistled, covering his thumb and middle finger in spit.

He offered them the stage of his place, The Quarter Arcade & Pool Hall, for the next weekend.

They played for a crowd of ten, three of which were old rancheros that looked as though they smelled something foul in the air when the three punks walked in with their equipment. Their scowls only intensified once the music started. The guitar was too distorted, the bass clicky. If they minded the drums, it wasn't evident, but the guitars were so loud that the percussion was as mild as a gentle knock on the door. Their antics had most of the Quarter Arcade staring at them as though all of it were some godless ritual. Thrash ran around the stage, eyes blacked out in homage to Doyle Wolfgang von Frankenstein, and yelled into the microphone, slamming his head against it until he bled. He smeared the blood on the guitar strings and spat on the floor. All of it was done with a practiced sneer.

But, it wasn't until "Fuck Your Horse, Fuck This Town" that the crowd turned on them. At first, it was only a few boos from the dark edges of the venue. A few calls of 'fags' and 'freaks.' But, when one of the old rancheros tossed a beer bottle their way, it was the start of a flood. The crowd tossed bottles, pennies, soggy bar pretzels, and pool balls at them. Yet, they played all the same, muscling through "Hunt for the Lechuza" before a bottle thudded against Thrash's guitar.

In the middle of a song, Thrash picked up the bottle and shouted, "What the fuck do you damn pig-fucking inbreds know about music?" He chucked the bottle at the table of rancheros, who didn't hesitate to go for their pocket-knives. They left in a hurry, Thrash and Travieso swinging their instruments like clubs, carving a path to their van.

Manoplas de Dios had to go back the next day to get Travieso's drum set. Someone had slashed the drumheads.

"Well," Thrash said, crossing his arms over his Crass shirt. "I still think it was Rob's fault."

"Then what about Asheville?" Grosero said. He coughed onto the denim vest he wore which was covered in sewn-on patches and studded spikes. "I was healthy as a horse in Asheville."

In Asheville, the trio lined up a gig on a rickety stage in the backroom of Sam's Pizza Joint. Halfway into "And You Call Me a Freak," Grosero vomited onto one of their small amps, sending stinking sparks out across the floor, stinging the few drunk women who left their vaqueros and beer-soaked husbands to get a closer look at the three punks. The smell of curdling vomit cleared the restaurant, which now was hardly frequented on account of the lingering stench.

Thrash scoffed. "You've never been healthy a day in your life. I heard you gave your mother the clap on your way out."

"And I gave it to yours on the way in," Grosero said, pumping his hips at the singer.

"Is that a fact, *Robert?*" a woman's voice said from the door leading into the house. Mrs. Offenbach, a heavy-set woman in her forties, stood there wearing her work clothes, a set of stained overalls.

At the sight of her, Grosero sneezed as though the sight of his sickness might exempt him from any retort.

"Don't you think I'd remember a needle-dicked shit-for-brains grunting on top of me," she said, glaring at him. "Now, you kids go home. You scared my dogs enough with that racket. Rafa, you tell your mother I said hello," she told Travieso. "Oh, and Rob, go to the damn doctor. I feel like I'm going to get the plague just looking at you."

"Sure thing, Mrs. O," Grosero told her.

II.

The three of them were an unwelcome sight on the streets of San Casimiro, drawing stares and laughter. Rosita's wouldn't let them eat there anymore since Pedro Lucio and his bunch broke two tables and a dozen plates fighting the three of them. The bartender, Ibañez, let them order food if they picked it up around back. To pass the time between practices, they usually found themselves at the old cattle stockyards, forty years abandoned.

The place was overrun with weeds and shrub trees, vines creeping up the ruined walls until bits of green pushed out from under the slanted roof as if some long-outdated spacecraft had fallen to Earth to be devoured by dirt. Under the sloping roof was a network of corrals with doors rusted from their hinges. Cigarette butts and countless beer cans littered the dirt and weeds. Past these was a single staircase that led to the offices, which overlooked the entire yard. To each side of the offices were catwalks dangling from rusted wire that swayed and groaned with the slightest breeze. With the monstrous roar of the old catwalks rattling the office walls, Thrash sat on a wobbly stool and passed a half-smoked joint to Travieso, who used a marker to draw the band's symbol: brass knuckles with an upside down cross for a middle finger.

Grosero smoked from a pipe since the others didn't want his perpetual cold.

"Thing is, man, we got to line up gigs to push the record," Thrash said through a cough. "I've got three hundred copies of *Broken Teeth* fucking melting in my house."

"Problem is location," Travieso said as he inhaled a lungful of smoke. In a strained voice, he went on. "No place with the right crowd since everyone who's anyone in the scene is at--" He coughed for a long time, then spat on the floor. "The Horned Toad. Up in Four Creeks. That's where we've got to be."

"Man," Grosero wheezed. "They won't even return our calls."

"Yeah," Thrash said. "Fucking dick Fito! All that guy likes is industrial shit with samples from old horror flicks. He doesn't get it. Not one damn bit."

"Why don't we get a sample then," Grosero offered. When they glared at him, Grosero shook his head. "Don't give me that look. I mean slap a song together with a sample, Zombie-style--"

"White or Rob?" Travieso asked, narrowing his eyes.

Grosero looked insulted. "White. But, put it in the background of like… 'Blood on the Tracks' or something and send it to him. Once we get there, we'll play that song first to get it out of the way. Even if we go into our normal stuff, Fito wouldn't cut a show short after only one song. *That* is what I'm saying."

"I think I figured it out," Thrash said, puffing on what was now a roach. "Rob here's got a brain tumor or something. Only way to explain being sick and getting smart at the same time."

As Grosero moved to send a jet of snot at Thrash, they heard the rumble of an engine and the crunch of tires on the loose gravel. From out the office window, due to the holes in the stockyard walls, the three of them saw a dented muscle car pull up the long drive and park out of sight of the road. Even at that distance, they could hear Pedro Lucio and his friends, Elmer and Rudy. All three were sons of San Casimiro, as Travieso often called them in a mocking tone. Content with living in dirt with the smell of cow shit lingering in the air, Pedro and the rest drank and fought to beat back the boredom. The vests and hair and piercings of *Manoplas de Dios* made them easy targets, since, for all they knew, they were the only punks for thirty miles.

Thrash told Travieso to leave the office and loop around the outer wall of the stockyard. Travieso was the biggest of them with forearms the size of calves and thick wrists. Travieso nodded and pulled the chain from around his waist before slinking away.

He wasn't gone a minute before a beer bottle shattered against the office door.

"Don't try hiding, *jotos*," Pedro called up. "I can hear Rob wheezing. I think you should give him a break. All that cock-sucking can't be good for his health." Pedro stood in the dirt, skirted by Elmer and Rudy, who laughed in a rehearsed, half-hearted way. When there was no response, Pedro scowled and opened his mouth to speak. "You guys--"

"If you three want to tug on each other, we'll go," Thrash said, sticking his head out of the broken office window. "Scout's honor, your secret's safe with us." A dusty bottle whizzed up at Thrash, but he didn't flinch. That was a sign of fear, something Thrash'd never show a son of San Casimiro.

The bottle broke above his head. Thrash smiled, not bothering to shake the brown glass from his hair.

"Come down here and say that, you pussy," Pedro shouted at them.

"Says the bastard who never starts a fight alone," Thrash laughed. "No thank you. But...," he said and reached into his back pocket, slipping his fingers into his set of brass knuckles. He tapped the metal against the window frame and smirked. "You're welcome to come up here. Just me and Rob."

Grosero sneezed and inhaled noisily.

"Where's the other one?" Elmer, a skinny track star with curly hair, called.

"Said he had a date with Lucio's mom," Thrash chuckled. "Bitch is so hairy I bet he's still looking for that pussy--" Thrash stopped when he saw Pedro move toward the walkway leading up to the office. He knew Pedro and his friends were capable of giving him a whipping, which they often did when they found one of the punks alone, but, with all the taunting, Pedro didn't notice Travieso walking quietly up to their backs, chain pulled taut to betray nothing of the plan.

Thrash went out of the office to meet them and Grosero followed, armed with nothing but his mucus crusted hands. Pedro smiled at them and clenched his fists, a fresh barrage of insults piling up in his throat. But, the sound of a chain rattling and Elmer grunting turned him around long enough for Thrash to plant a boot in the boy's chest, sending him tumbling down the walkway. Rudy was too shocked to do anything other than put his fists up, which did little when Grosero sneezed fully in his face. The three punks got him to the ground and kicked him a few times before escaping through the stockyard.

Halfway down the road, Thrash and Travieso stopped to wait for Grosero, who stumbled and skipped toward them while gulping at the air. He hawked up a discolored lump and spit it onto the cracked asphalt.

"We better go," Thrash told them, chewing on his lip ring. "That prick Lucio's bound to run us down if he finds us."

Thrash shook his head and started down the road. "Sons of San Casimiro, man," he said. "They're like fuckin' chickens. See one speck of difference and they want to kill it. But, you ask me, they need it."

"Need what?" Travieso asked.

"Us. People to judge, people to push down," Thrash told them. "While they're looking down on us, they don't have to give a good look at each other. Like we say: 'Watching the grass grow/ refusing to eat crow/ fillin' the dually with gas/ stuffing your big fat ass… and you call *me* the freak for standing up to speak.'"

Travieso nodded in silent agreement before stopping, as though realizing something. "Wait, we say that?"

"Yeah," Thrash replied.

"When?" Grosero asked, the words struggling past his clogged airways.

Thrash didn't stop walking. Shaking his head, he told them, "It's one of our songs."

"I don't write the lyrics," Travieso said, following Thrash. "Wouldn't that mean that you say it, not us."

Grosero, winded, told them to wait and, once he caught up to them, said, "To tell you the truth, I don't understand a fucking word you sing in any of our songs."

"That's punk, my friend," Thrash told them and, though they waited for him to follow it with something, their singer did not.

III.

Days later, east of town, they ate cold flautas from Rosita's out of styrofoam boxes. By the time they got there, the food was cold except for the *caldo de res* Ibañez packed for Grosero, who sipped at it reluctantly. "So, what's up, Rob?" Thrash asked, still chewing the crunchy tortilla. "You were so excited on the phone I thought you'd cough up a lung."

"Dude had me gagging from all the phlegm," Travieso agreed, spreading a lukewarm packet of sour cream onto one of the flautas. "Seriously, Rob, see a doctor."

Grosero sipped at his soup and took a deep breath. "I ran into my cousin yesterday," he started. "He came in to check on my grandpa."

"How's the old piece of shit doing?" Thrash asked.

"Crazy as ever, but at least they got him to wear pants," Grosero replied. "But, you know my cousin's in a band."

"*Dude*," Travieso whined. "He plays Simon and Garfunkel covers at the Holiday Inn in Laredo. I wouldn't call that a band."

"Doesn't matter," Grosero told him. "He was telling me there's a guy *in town* that has like a fucking shelf full of old tapes and shit."

"Who?" Thrash and Travieso asked.

"Of all people, fucking Jim Wetherwax," Grosero said.

"The Hermit?" Thrash said, using the town nickname for the heavy-set man who lived off Santos Road. He was an old bearded man with a few remaining teeth who only came to town once a month to buy toilet paper and porno mags. Some of the older folk said he'd wandered to San Casimiro to hone his witchcraft in the *monte*, where the spirits danced. Others said he was the former roadie for some psychedelic band long since separated. But, most people knew him as a suspected pedophile that occasionally sold weed of such poor quality, customers usually left with what looked like baggies of woodchips and dirt.

"The goddamn Hermit," Grosero confirmed. "I say we go over there with a couple of bucks and grab one. Record something with it and send the song to Fito."

"Nah," Travieso said. "That guy doesn't want cash. Only charges ten for a damn pillow of weed."

"Yeah," Thrash agreed. "Better to bring him a fucking chicken or something. Eat it or fuck it. His choice."

"When do you want to go see him?" Grosero asked.

"Let me steal a chicken from my grandma," Travieso said. "And, I'll meet you guys at Santos Road tomorrow."

"Sounds good," Thrash said, sopping up the bits of chicken with the last shreds of tortilla. "But, Rob, bring your old man's hunting knife just in case. Can't expect a warm welcome from anyone is this hellhole."

IV.

Santos Road ran parallel to a dried-out creek long overgrown with the withered roots of mesquite and yellowed cacti. Travieso walked in the center of it, kicking turtle shells with his steel-toed boots. They sounded like clay pots and the dust from them puffed in the stale air. Thrash carried the old hen in a birdcage of domed wired as Grosero teared up and sneezed every few steps.

Travieso howled in delight and ran to a set of old, white Brehma bones. The drummer fell to his knees and dug around the skull until he could slide it out by the two curved horns. He presented it to the other, loose dirt pouring from the missing lower jaw. "Check it out," he said, lifting it as he examined the skull. "I bet with some wires and a bit of tape, this'll make a cool mask. I'll wear it during shows."

"Man," Thrash scoffed. "All you'll do is get a scalp full of mites. Get out of there already." He gestured ahead of them. The Hermit's house sat about a half a mile up the road, surrounded by blooming huisache.

It was little more than a one room shack of corrugated metal sheets and steel pipes set into a cement foundation. Every piece of metal was fringed in rust. On the tips of the crude roof were chimes comprised of the small bones of jackrabbits and rattlesnakes. Behind the house, covered by the semicircle of huisache trees sat a dozen budding marijuana plants. The Hermit left them out in the open, rumor had it, because he tied rattlers to the stems in case anyone tried to steal his crop. But, as the trio of punks knew, kids from their high school grew better stuff.

The three of them assumed gruff poses when Thrash knocked on the tattered screen door.

From inside the shack, they heard a radio turned down. A hoarse voice snarled something.

Jim Wetherwax filled the doorframe when he opened it. He was a bearded man with ice water blue eyes. In his wiry beard were the stains of pipe resin and salsa. Spit and tobacco juice. "I'd make a Halloween joke but… I'd imagine you've already heard it," he said after a silent minute passed.

"Got it once this morning," Thrash said.

"Why do you have a chicken?" the Hermit asked.

"Figured you'd have use for one," Thrash said.

The others crossed their arms.

"Never traded weed for a chicken before," the Hermit said, leaning against the doorframe.

"As much as we'd like some," Thrash told him. "We're here for something else. We heard you've got a shit load of old recordings. Samples and stuff."

"Got some sitting in a box, yeah," the Hermit said. "Come on in. I'll put a few on. But," he said and held out his pudgy hand. The fingers were stained an odd color. "He can't bring that cow skull in here. One mite gets in my place, I'll die from scratching."

Inside, the space was filled with a cluttered picnic table too close to the sink and fridge a few feet from the cot the Hermit soiled nightly. On a small table, a static-filled stereo whispered some Hank Williams tune. The Hermit shuffled towards the table and slid a beaten cardboard box from under it and placed it on the counter, where Thrash had put the old hen.

"Mind if I smoke?" Travieso asked, dusty hands reaching into his vest pocket.

"Nope?" the Hermit replied before lighting one of his own. "Well, there's what I got. Found that shit when I moved in. The old tenant was the one who recorded them or collected them. Some science guy, I think. I don't know. Pick out whichever. What do you boys need that junk for anyhow?"

"Need a quick gimmick to get a show lined up," Grosero said, wiping his nose with his sleeve.

Thrash went through the box, discarding old country legend B-sides or tapes marked with the titles of classic books by middle class women. Near the end of his search, he found a cassette marked *Roadrunner Sessions 2 & 3* in an almost razor-like script. "Hey," he said to the others. "Let's put this one on, see what it sounds like."

The Hermit walked the tape over to the radio and jammed it into the deck.

The trio sat and smoked cigarettes as the static faded…

———•———

'…*the date… is unimportant. My name is Dr. Dante Rinaldi and I am about to have my second attempted conversation with my new friend… can you say your name for the recorder?*'

There was only a hissing breath in response.

'*Forgive my guest,*' *the voice went on.* '*Erronymous is its true name, but he is rather angry with me today… because I tricked you, yes?*'

A throaty growl vibrated onto the tape.

'*Well, it's true, yes?*' *the doctor said.* '*You regret telling me your true name in a drunken haze. But, do not blame me for your mistakes that day… To think of you then is truly… amazing. You had the form of a flightless bird then, yes? To think this twisted visage looming beneath it… just amazing. More boar than winged ape, I say. But, there is a hint of the buzzard in you. There is still one thing you will not give up, yes? A thing the old books rave about. The masters, Nikodemus and the Marquis de Mammon. Even for the Archibald of Gloutshire, that plagiarist, did one of your kind open the doors.*'

The wood of an old chair groaned.

'*You know what it is, Erronymous.*'

There was a low grunt and shrill peal of a startled pig.

'*Speak… speak for me. Speak so that I may know.*'

A groan.

'Erronymous, speak for me,' the doctor said in a slow monotone, a metro-nome against the sounds of whatever thing he loosely controlled... 'Come now, Erronymous,' the doctor said.

At the sound of its name, the creature yelped as though gripped suddenly by a terrible force.

'Speak to me,' the doctor cooed. 'Share with me all the knowledge buried in that horrid skull. The sights from the edge of reality itself. Tell me of the grotesque machinations that formed you, Erronymous.'

It roared at him with the coupled voices of pig and ape.

'You hold out because of your vanity,' the doctor accused. 'But... you will speak. I've read the books of the outer dark... learned their ways. You will speak and I will know.'

The creature grew quiet.

'Speak to me... speak Erronymous... I am your master and I command you to speak...'

———◆———

After the doctor on the tape repeated the order a few times, there were min-utes of static-filled silence. The Hermit only asked for five dollars. Thrash bought it and a nickel bag of what could have been tobacco, and the three of them left. They agreed the tape sounded like a cheap knockoff of a Vincent Price monologue, but they felt a gutter-eared asshole like Fito would think it sounded great.

Travieso spliced it with "Cow Shit in the Air (A Love Song)" and deliv-ered it to Fito in Four Creeks alone. It was a short drive, one that afforded the drummer a chance to give the original tape a thorough study. Punk music, he often thought, doesn't have to sound like a cranky junky raping a speaker with an out-of-tune guitar. The speech was slow enough to fit something into, but listening to it, Travieso was glad he only had to do it once.

The doctor hadn't stopped speaking but for a few minutes before the stocky drummer pulled up to the front of the Horned Toad, where a brown skinned old man sat dozing with a beer at his feet. It was a squat wooden building covered in old advertisements long-degraded and rusted obscure, but on the front of the door was a crudely painted Horned Toad, Xs over its eyes, empty mug in hand. Inside, the cement floor had enough room for sixty people and the bar along the wall sat an additional seven. Fito, Travieso knew, would be smoking on the last stool, drunk.

Hoping to be quick, Travieso didn't bother turning off the van, leaving the tape to drone on in its tuneless static.

After a long time, there was a growl on the tape. A throbbing sneer and Erronymous said, *yad siht rof ssenevigrof ym geb lliw uoy neht… em ot uoy evig lliw erif eht htaeneb sllewd ohw eno eht, semoc emit ruoy nehw.*

The tape ended with laughter. Both doctor's and demon's.

The old drunk napping in the sun woke with a sudden jerk of his shoulders. He looked around, trying to see what might have woken him. But, other than the van nearby or the grackles coughing in the trees, there was nothing there. He sat there with his eyes focused on the lonely road in front of him. Then, his eyes narrowed. A notion overcame him like a revelation, some unexplainable force. He stood, knocking over his beer, and stepped toward the road. Though he'd lived in Four Creeks for years, the old drunk looked at the long stretch of asphalt like it was trespassing on his sacred ground. In the distance, a truck bounced down the road. The sight of it angered the man, and he didn't know why. But, all his thoughts were to destroying that truck, that metal vagrant wantonly parading around where it didn't belong, kicking up stones and farting out gasses. Enraged, the old drunk waited until the truck was close before pouncing in front of it.

———◆———

Travieso found Thrash sweeping out his parent's garage the next day. Thrash leaned the broom against a set of dusty shelves and looked around before he lit a cigarette. "Any word?" he asked and offered his pack of smokes to his friend. Travieso took one and lit it.

"Yep," Travieso said. "Got the call and came over here…" He looked out to the street. Off in the distance, an old man drowned a gardenia bush with his hose as he stared at them.

149

"Don't even say it," Thrash said. "That prick wouldn't know--"

Travieso's apish face morphed into that of a grinning idiot. "All I can say is thank god I took a picture of that old drunk smeared on the highway. It'll look good on the flyer."

"No fucking way," Thrash said, letting a momentary bit of excitement into his voice before resuming his indifferent attitude.

"The gig's on a Thursday, so don't get too excited," the drummer chuckled. "Said if he likes what he sees, we'll get to open once a month. But, he's sure as shit going to hate us."

"It's up to the people, my man," Thrash said, taking a long drag off his cigarette. "They decide the bands they want to hear. Fuck Fito. If we get that place to go wild, that'll be that."

Travieso nodded and smoked. "You heard from Rob today? I went by his place earlier, but the car was gone."

"Off to see some city doctor," Thrash said. "Apparently, he sneezed on a dog and it damn collapsed. Hope they don't quarantine him. Hey!" Thrash said, snapping his fingers. "Do you have the tape? I figure we might as well keep it in the stereo until the show. I'll make sure it gets there all right."

"Yeah," Travieso said. "Just have to rewind it. Might take a bit to find--"

"Doesn't even matter," Thrash told him. "Just leave like fifteen minutes on the tape. You know, the shit about knowledge and the banishment and all that. It's just got to sound creepy, you know. Once that plays, we can drone it out with something pure. Something this fucking town needs."

"Nothing like a little punk to cure what ails you," he said. He walked to the truck to get the tape.

The tape sat in the stereo for a week, unplayed. Grosero returned from the city, having had dozens of examinations that did little other than put all the nurses who handled his blood samples in the ICU. The band complete once more, *Manoplas de Dios* practiced the entire set of songs off *Broken Teeth* and even wrote a two-minute song titled "This Town Burning at My Back" for the occasion. Even apart, they practiced as though it were a ritual, a duty to the unseen elder gods of punk. That week, they fought sons of San Casimiro like the champions of Greek epics. They strode the streets boldly, eyes set like creatures possessed with a single intent. And through it all, they left the tape untouched, playing it briefly only to check the stereo's batteries.

The night of the show, Thrash set the stereo at the edge of the stage as they set up their instruments. Dressed in his leathers, a *Manoplas de Dios* emblem on the back-patch, Thrash sized up the small crowd. Most were older and covered in faded jailhouse ink. Some of the county-scene kids stood there with their piercings and ironed shirts emblazoned with the faces of Jello Biafra and Ian Curtis as though part of their musical tribe. Fito himself, a short pot-bellied man with a small goatee and yellow tinted sunglasses, sat at the bar with a smoldering cigar between his teeth and a chubby rockabilly girl on his arm.

Grosero put on a carpenter's mask painted to resemble fangs and plugged in his bass. Thrash pressed the pedal of his high-hats to test them. Once ready, he nodded from behind his drum set, spray painted with the logo of *Manoplas de Dios*. Thrash nodded back and stepped up to his microphone, the sides of his shaven head glistening in the spotlight. The crimson mohawk he wore was a special thing, his cockscomb of defiance. Sneering, he said, "Four Creeks! We're *Manoplas de Dios*! And this one's a little love song I wrote! 'Cow Shit in the Air!'"

He nudged the play button on the stereo as Travieso opened with a rapid beat. The trio played despite the tape, uncaring about a coherent mixture of sounds. Thrash screamed over the doctor's raspy voice, barked over the animal sounds of Erronymous. The guitar players bucked wildly, gyrating like fools and stomping on the stage until the song was over. The tape spoke briefly during the transition to "Broken Teeth, Sour Apples." It was Dr. Rinaldi whispering about machinations on the edge of reality.

In that short space, *Manoplas de Dios* noticed Fito scowl before making his way toward them. But, Thrash wouldn't give him the space to pull them off the stage, shouting the title of some song and jumping into it.

It was halfway through "Sons of San Casimiro, Fuck You" that a few people bobbed their heads and the drunk truckers threw up their fist, though it wasn't clear whether it was out of genuine enjoyment or cruel mockery. Even that small movement, that tiny approval, filled the band's lungs with a sweet wind of victory. "All right Horned Toad," Thrash shouted down at them. "We wrote this song just for you. It's called 'Leaving With This Town Burning at

My Back!'" He turned and gestured at Travieso with his chin. The beat was a slow one that was dominated by snare and bass drum, but beneath the sound of it, hidden by a torrent of the same three chords, Erronymous growled his unholy glossolalia: "*Yad siht rof ssenevigrof ym geb lliw uoy neht... em ot uoy evig lliw erif eht htaeneb sllewd ohw eno eht, semoc emit ruoy nehw.*"

On stage, on the ground, the song seemed to whip everyone into a frenzy. The scene-kids pushed and shoved one another with gusto, sending one through a window. When Fito went over to the band, pointing and shouting about their set, Thrash, amid his singing, felt a strange urge well up inside him. For all the talk of hating Fito and all the man stood for, the three punks had never really meant to do him any harm, despite their big talk. Yet, as the stubby man approached the stage, swinging his finger back and forth, Thrash snarled into the microphone like a cornered animal. As Fito reached the stage, Thrash let his guitar hang from his shoulder. He bellowed some indecipherable words and swung the microphone like a club. The metal mesh thudded loudly against Fito's skull and tore his forehead. Thrash raised the microphone and struck Fito again.

The stubby club-owner tried to backtrack from the maniacal singer, but found a vise grip of flesh on the front of his shirt. Before he could put up any resistance, Thrash pulled the man on stage and tossed the microphone aside. His shouts into the face of Fito kept to the tempo of the song, so the scene-kids continued in their play despite the man bleeding on stage. If anything, the violence set before them seemed to make them crazed. They threw bottles on stage, fought in pockets, and howled at the ceiling like dogs.

A bottle broke beside Thrash, breaking his fanatic concentration. As if struck by some divine inspiration, Thrash took hold of the broken bottle neck and slashed Fito across his cheeks over and over again. With each swing, a bit of the bottle buried itself into Fito's skin and broke off until Thrash was doing little more than slapping the man with his open hand, which bled from green slivers of glass embedded into it. He found himself repeating words to which he knew had no meaning.

The band played on.

Thrash tore into the man laid out before him, digging into the soft flesh of his stomach with clawed fingers and ripping through it with an inhuman strength. Once the man was opened up, the singer set to throwing the ropey innards in gleaming handfuls to the crowd and to his band mates. Some of the people closest to the stage screamed in terror and ran, only to be chased away by the growing population of lunatics in the small venue. Even with the music fast and loud, the sounds of madmen descending on others was evident. Out there, beyond the stage, people fell under dozens of hands to be beaten with chunks of asphalt or steel-toed boots.

In the distance, sirens wailed. People scattered to evade them or stood to face the sheriffs like warriors of a dead age.

Inside, Thrash was elbows deep in Fito's open stomach. There was nothing left in there but blood and bones he couldn't tear free. His fingers were too slick with blood, too shredded by glass. But, the sirens sang to him like the angelic voices of saviors. He wiped the sweat from his brow, oblivious to the slivers of glass cut deep lines into his skin. He looked out into the Horned Toad, empty save for a few bodies stripped naked and swollen from bruises. He moved his ruined finger across his throat, telling Rob and Travieso to stop the music. The band stopped playing and looked up at the empty room as though they had awakened from a dream.

The sirens drew closer.

Thrash smiled and laughed in a low tone. He hopped off the stage and picked up a bottle that had been thrown but not broken. Thrash smashed its end against the stage. "You hear that, boys," he asked the band, pointing outside with his bloody hand. "That's the sound of change. That's the sound of San Casimiro dying."

Grosero and Travieso nodded, the same wild eyes narrowing on their faces. The sirens reached their crescendo, blaring a few feet from outside the door. Shots were fired at the shouting crowd, but no one dispersed. More shots. A cluster of the crazed crowd climbed onto the cruisers and scrapped in the dirt.

Manoplas de Dios stood in the empty place, fists clenched and jaws set, ready to meet what was outside of the Horned Toad.

—ETC.—

La Boda

Before the cressets were extinguished and all the light stolen, she saw the knowing stares of the blind priestesses and the ceremonial tools and garments in their wrinkled hands. The darkness was cold against her skin. The blind priestesses came at her like a murder of crows, tugging at her hair and pulling at her nakedness. They felt her, sensed her, for the first time since asking to take her from her father's home. They combed the dirt of peasant life from her hair, sprinkling it with oils that made the air smell of wildflowers. They shaved her with chips of obsidian pressed between their fingers.

When she jumped, they were quick to stop, flaring away like flies before returning to their work. "Hold still, now," they'd say. "He wants you whole. The bleeding is his to do."

They bathed her in fragrant waters, whispers of prayer and the fingertips of blessing prodding her. Their touch sickened her, but she knew that to be born into that land was to be born into a covenant. To some, her upcoming marriage was a badge of honor, though in that utter darkness it felt more like a grave. She'd expected shadow, but in the catacombs beneath San Angosto de la Tierra, that darkness had a smell, a touch that groped at her in a way more upsetting than that of the priestesses.

She wondered if he was handsome. If he would be kind or cruel. Those same thoughts had kept her awake at night, caused her to eat little and speak even less.

The priestesses dressed her blessed body as though it were a mannequin. They lifted her arms, her breath sucking loudly when the inner-lining of the corset touched her naked flesh, and squeezed her until she thought she might topple over. They tugged at her ankles as though shoeing a horse and slid on her undergarments, fixing and smoothing them with their dry hands. Next came the heavy patchwork gown, the same one used over and over, the shreds of it collected once he was done removing them from his brides. Its heft blended with the gloom and the suffocating feel of the corset. The whispered prayers made her dizzy, but the blind priestesses went about their work despite her swaying.

She was primped and powdered and manicured. Treated in ways she'd never known in her peasant's life, one of toil and infrequent meals. She knew once the blind priestesses came to her father's door with His request for her hand, a new life awaited her and her family.

It was an honor, the priestesses insisted.

"It is important," once of the priestesses said behind her. "That when he looks at you that you not look away. He'll not strike you blind, child. Unlike us, he will allow you to gaze upon him. He desires it."

"How will I know him?" she asked.

After a long moment, a voice rasped, "Don't be foolish, child. You'll know him. You'll not be able to ignore his nobility."

"How can you say that about what you've never seen?" she asked.

"I saw him once…," the voice said. "A most generous of gift and the last true sight I ever had." There was yearning mingled with the words.

They decked her fingers with rings with heavy stones set into the metalwork and they weighed down her neck with necklaces of what felt like bones. The priestesses clasped bracelets of gold around her ankles and wrists. At the sound of the last click, the voices of the priestesses stopped and it felt to the woman, for one impossible second, that she was in that subterranean room alone before she felt their old hands turning her toward the door. They led her out of it into the corridors, which had also been darkened in preparation of her arrival.

He was to be the first thing his newly cleansed bride would see.

Surrounding her, they led her down the corridor, the path's gentle downward slope spiraling in a gradual loop. They walked in silence, the priestesses out reverence to their lord and her out of anxiety. After many minutes, a wall of hands stopped her.

"May his blessings upon you number among the infinite," a new voice said. The priestesses moved aside.

With them out of her path, she felt that she was in front of a large door. A dull but bouncing light spilled at her feet. So long had she been in darkness, even the flames of the candles, though hundreds, struck her eyes like tiny suns.

The room was a holy place in the heart of the earth, the natural ceiling stained black from the centuries of ceremonies preformed there. The unions that began before her town was a village. Before even the land was tamed. All about the chamber were candelabras whose lights cast a noxious smell that warmed the room and made her head swim. Yet, even with the wavering sights of lights and smoke, the girl knew the priestesses' words to be true: she knew him the instant she entered the sacred chambers.

She smiled for he had kind eyes.

He was not so terrible, not such a horror as the stories told. The curved horns about his temples gave him a regal air and the muscles of his hulking form were more pleasant than repulsive, despite the sharpened growths of bone and ivory jutting through it, proof of some cosmic ritual of mutilation. And she'd seen no finer cloak than the leathery wings he wore about its uncovered nethers. She felt a wave of relief, almost comedy, at the thought of those stories she'd heard growing up, tales spun by frightened farmers and their wives. His talons did not frighten her. They beckoned her to something greater than humanity--to an appreciation of existence incomprehensible.

It was not every day that a peasant girl would wed a god.

—ETC.—

THE HUNGRY MAN SEES FAR

for Charlie

The Man slurped his microwaveable chicken curry off the blue plastic fork with the edges of his mouth upturned in a sharp grin of delight. His giggles came out of him like ecstatic smoke rings. Three sailors watched him and said nothing to the Man, who had wrapped in a blanket that he wore like a shredded cape. "Mmmm...," the Man hummed before bringing another sloppy spoonful to his unshaven face. His hair stuck out at odd ends from all around his cranium and nape, tossed along with his mushy bulk as he sucked on the tines.

"So, uh, how's it taste?" one of the sailors asked.

As if only now noticing his audience sitting around the filthy lo mein-splattered table, his eyes shot up and narrowed like a lion's in sight of scavengers. Reflexively, he closed his sun-dried hands around the black plastic plate despite the heat and considered the question. "It tastes like freedom," the Man said.

———◆———

Oh, they'll never think I'll be hiding here, the Man thought as he gripped his hairy belly all the tighter to conceal its deep rumblings. He pressed his back harder against the Cooking Rock--a giant flat stone used by the village--and scowled at the east, to Africa, a place he hated for its food, and then shook his head at the thought of the west and all the Middle Eastern delights that never made their way to his village. Always the grand warlord, Ploombana the Brutal, and his scores of dope-fed child soldiers took the frozen cuisines at the border and microwaved them with the supply of beautiful machines they'd stolen from the people of his village. In remembrance of the little bell that chimed whenever his TV dinners were ready and steaming with exotic aromas, his belly complained. The Man punched his belly into a temporary silence. He'd named his microwave Marvin and it was the most exquisite microwave in the entire village, even though he had to use a gutted exercise-bike to generate the power it needed. But, the food had always been evenly cooked and worth the trouble.

"He doesn't need that many microwaves. He doesn't need Marvin," the Man whispered to himself, but he quickly slapped his hands onto his dry mouth when he heard the approach of someone wanting to use the Cooking Rock, which warmed with the sun that seemed to loom only a few feet from the tops of the thatch roofs of his home. Some days, the Man felt he could reach out and touch the fiery orb. He pulled his prized possession, a simple blue blanket, around him to conceal himself further. The foot falls grew closer and it took all of him not to giggle in anticipation. He sniffed the air in hopes of catching his next meal's scent, but all that flooded his nostrils was the dry stink of hungry, frozen-dinner deprived people he regrettably called neighbors.

They let Ploombana the Brutal take his precious Marvin and its bubbled, lime green door that seemed to rejoice every time it cooked, spinning the black trays round and round in the golden light of ingenuity. A frown replaced his childlike laughter and nearly sent him into a fit of cursing, but the odd sound behind him pulled his eyelids to his bushy brows and cheeks. The hard clunk atop the Cooking Rock sounded like, though it surely couldn't have been, a frozen tray. He dared not look, not yet. With his hand pressed against his mouth, he let out a meow--a call he practiced nightly--and his shoulders tensed in anticipation.

The footsteps did not move.

With a furrowed brow, he let out the same meek noise, but louder. "Kitty?" a little girl's voice chimed.

His smile went to his ears and the Man mewed again, letting the shrill note last for a moment before killing it. The sound of dry dirt crunching under shoddy sandals sang to him, and his shoulders bounced in silent musing.

"Here kitty, kitty," the girl said, and, from the sounds of her feet, she was halfway around the large, flat Cooking Rock. "Do you want something to eat?" the girl said.

She was so close, the Man could smell her.

The girl's tiny brown face peeked around the rock with eyes wide and smile hopeful.

"Bwaagagagah!" the Man screamed as he sprung up like a great bird, waving his hands above his head quickly. He shot up raving, and the little girl's tiny, thin legs couldn't carry her away fast enough. So, frightened, she didn't dare look back as the Man continued his madness, stomping his bare feet in the dust as if the very dirt was granular fire while his tongue lolled out his head and both his eyes crossed and split like searchlights until she rounded the dry copse of trees towards the village, shouting of monsters and trolls and any other creature her parents swore would eat her if she didn't sleep when commanded.

The Man laughed at the sight of the dust settling from her mad sprint, but he knew he couldn't enjoy it for long. The villagers would come and probably beat him with spades and sticks for shocking the little girl. He turned to the Cooking Rock and felt the tears well up in his eyes at the sight of frozen chicken curry with its gravy cubes glistening like a dozen tiny mirrors that showed nothing but sparkling delight. His hairy belly heaved; he aimed his laugh at the skies, and it was loud. With careful hands, he picked up the lukewarm container, speeding it away to some nearby bushes, where he often hid himself from the dimwittedness of the fellows who let his precious Marvin be collected at gunpoint and hauled off like a screaming child into the vast Betty Crocker collection of Ploombana the Brutal's halls.

He carefully lifted the thin plastic cover from it, taking care not to rip the elegant sheet. The scent, the sight, had his mouth spilling over, but he found he couldn't eat. As he brought it to his face, the idea of eating the semi-frozen meal repulsed him, making his already crabby gut growl like a pissy cat. "I know," he said to it. "We must eat this right. That is the problem. Things are done. But, they are not done right." He shot up, taking several small branches with him, and with a deep breath, dared to speak the madness of his plan aloud: "I must microwave!" He looked around, but no one was near. Bringing the curry to him like a tiny wounded animal, he whispered, "I'll eat you far from this place. A place of destinies. Where you'll be warm and tasty and cooked." He smashed the stuff to his hairy chest, winced, and ran further into the forest, knowing well how to reach the edge of Ploombana the Brutal's tyrannical grip.

———◆———

He went through the forest with the freezing plate high over his head, letting the sun warm his meal in the absence of Marvin, being careful to mind the rocks and thick roots that threatened to stub his toes and compromise his meal. The wooden gates were wrapped in rusty barbed wire. A few scalps dangled from the rusty wire. Old cars had been overturned to make walls for soldiers to hide behind. Waiting to see what manner of guards went in and out of their rounds, the Man murmured sweet reassurances to his hungry gut and to his precious meal, which seemed to call to him. He brought it close to his ear, but the sound of a young boy humming a tune broke the moment and brought a scowl to his face.

The skinny kid, semi-automatic rifle slung over one shoulder, goose-stepped to his own beat with a hand-rolled cigarette sticking to his young lips. A peace-sign was prominent on the stock of the weapon. He smiled when no other soldier came into his sight. The boy was alone and oblivious. Without another thought, the Man grabbed a dried stick. He waited until the boy came closer, taking deep drags of his Ploombana the Brutal issued tobacco, and when he turned on his heel to continue his mindless to and fro, the Man leapt at him. The stick whipped through the air, breaking on top of the boy's large, round head with a loud crack. "What the hell!" the kid screamed, rubbing his head vigorously. "Are you crazy?"

The Man widened his stance and used the broken stick like a pointing finger. "You'll not keep me in this place, foul boy! I'll eat my meal where I damn well please--"

"Who's stopping ya?"

"Not all the guns, not all the bullets, will keep me here to be befouled by Plumbana the Brutal's stubby member of injustice!"

"Gun ain't loaded."

"Shoot me if you will--"

"With what? The gun isn't loaded, you daffy bastard!" the kid yelled and showed him the empty magazine, but the Man was ranting to the skies. He bolted through the gate with his plate as high as his girlish laugh. "Goddamn! Crazy bastard," the kid spat, shrugging his shoulders. He continued his song and march until a uniformed soldier returned from behind the tiny shed that acted as a gate post. The kid clasped his belt and whistled long into his walk.

"You ever shit a hydra, kid? Cut off one, then two more come out," he laughed. "Thanks for holding my gun." He took it and reloaded the live rounds into it. "So, anyone try to get out?"

The kid shook his head, which the soldier rubbed with his hand.

"You got a weird bump on your noggin, kid. Get knocked around much?" the soldier laughed. He told the child to go play with the dirt, the communal toy of the village that none of them were greedy enough to horde.

———◆———

Despite the sharp burrs digging into his calloused heels and clinging like stowaways to his thick leg hair, the Man walked further into the dense forest, keeping the chilled plate above his head to be warmed by the last glimmers of sunlight. Soon, the trees grew further apart and sharp rocks knocked against his bare feet instead of twisting roots.

At the edge of the forest, he stopped, bit down on his coveted meal's plastic dish, and tied his blue blanket around his head, letting it drape across his shoulders like a dyed mane. He looked out to the rolling desert that blew hot, stinging gusts filled with specks of sand into his eyes, then lifted his plate towards the sky and walked opposite the sun's descent towards what his stomach assured him was Marvin's birthplace, a land where men could appreciate a microwave more for keeping time or sitting near, if only to be amused by the warm hum of its radiation.

The sand burnt his naked feet and rubbed the skin raw with each step, which never faltered no matter the steep dunes he had to climb with one hand above his head. The heat bore down on his limbs like unseen fire that snaked its way through the coarse hairs of his arms and torso, scorching his belly red. Every time he reached the top of a mountainous dune, the Man put the cool plate to his brow, letting the cast shadow allow his eyes to map out his route through the endlessly barren sands that had massive stones jutting out of the fine dust like craggy teeth of some devil long killed and stained by the wind that stole the water from the Man's mouth instead of the sight from his eyes.

In some way, he was thankful. The sun dipped low in the sky, but the thought of his meal kept his feet working tirelessly as they had when he needed their strength to pedal his bicycle generator for Marvin.

I have to forget Marvin, he thought. *I'll never go back. Never!*

The mere thought of Marvin cooking for that bastard Ploombana the Brutal sent a lonely tear, all his body could spare, down his face. The sand clung to it like a thousand thirsty hands of shattered stone; when he moved to wipe it, the tiny grains dug a deep scratch into his cheek. Yet, with feet weighed down by ankle-deep earth, he went forward through the night, picking his way only by the starlight and a half-moon that looked down on him with a cartoonish grin, which he would have spat at had he the saliva to spare; he couldn't stand anything laughing at his expense, heavenly body or not.

He only paused to wrap his blanket around his shoulders, placing his untouched meal close to his heart. The night was cold, and it would be foolish to let the meal freeze again. The chill stung his chest, but he endured it. The Man had to.

In the night, the meal froze.

———◆———

The colors of the sunrise, which painted the sky in rich purples and lively pinks, were lost on him; all it moved was his arm into the position of a flesh pillar topped with a flat hand displaying his plate to the gods above. The Man moaned about his thirst, but only the wind answered him, stealing moisture from his open maw then blowing away to scatter his complaints for miles. "So thirsty," he repeated. His tongue had grown fat and rough, each taste bud feeling like a pebble gritting against his teeth and cutting the roof of his mouth. As if in conversation, his growling stomach sounded like it was deflating inside his hairy skin with squishing noises and the creaking of old wood. He closed his fist to silence it, but he lacked the strength to strike himself, settling for one word: "Quiet!" And even that was half-hearted and strained.

Closing his eyes, he trudged through mountains of endless sand, listening to his feet sift through the grains with hisses and crunches. Then the Man heard it. At first, he thought it was his own organs pumping, but the tiny sound beat too fast to be his own failing heart. Weakly, he looked to the horizons all around him but saw nothing save a few vultures in the sky. He lifted his foot, dismissing the auditory mirage to half-starved madness, but the sound beat louder in his ears, turning his head all about until it settled on the tiny, sand colored drummer. The gecko looked up at him with eyes two sizes bigger than its face should've allowed and cocked its flat head as it blinked up at him.

The Man giggled through his pursed lips, and the little lizard quickly moved its limbs to stare up at him straight. He carefully unwrapped his blue blanket, placing his meal inside it like a treasure, and stooped to drop it on the soft earth, being careful not to move too quickly. With each movement, he heard the tiny creature's heart pumping wildly, though its little frame made no show of fear, only curiosity. Both of his meaty hands went out wide as if he prepared for a wild applause; the gecko didn't move save blinking. The big man sprang forward, slapping his cupped hands together with a spray of sand and an excited grunt. The Man lifted his hands above his head and looked around for any sign of movement, but nothing stirred the sands other than the undying wind.

He peered into his hands by spreading his thumbs wide enough for a slit. He couldn't see anything, but he felt the lizard wriggle inside his fingers. The Man squealed with delight. The Man shook his hands wildly, feeling a tiny reptile bounce around the flesh bars, sending the bits of sand flying all around him like a fine sacred salt. He opened his hands, looked at the dazed creature, and took him up with two pinching digits. He stared into its loopy eyes for a moment, then bit off its head and spat it out on the sand. He sucked on the neck, letting the rich drops of blood trickle into his mouth as he squeezed it from tail to forelegs like a ketchup packet. Repeating the action yielded foul tasting juices. Soon, there was nothing left in the Man's hands save a paper-thin husk of a gecko, which he tossed over his shoulder like a piece of rubbish.

The cool, refreshing blood seemed to clear his sight; the ground was populated with the small lizards, and he kicked up puffs of wispy sand as he caught one after the other in his shaking hands. With each, he tore off their confused heads, squeezed their tiny bodies, squirting sustenance into his openly joyous mouth. The rich liquor collected in thin streams at the back of his throat, but he couldn't seem to get enough and took up another and another, gorging his parched throat with the thin red lines that pumped quickly through their spasm-ridden bodies. If he'd been there for days or hours or minutes, he couldn't tell and didn't care to. All that mattered was the red droplets that clung to the corners of his mouth.

Buzzed on blood, surrounded by little headless carcasses, the Man finally took up his precious meal and smacked his refreshed lips together. His vigorous steps, like that of the child soldier he'd bested, scared dozens of the creatures into hiding under rocks or burrowing under a thin layer of sand, only letting their rounded black eyes peek out to watch the giant tramp onward.

The Hungry Man Sees Far

The sun rose to its apex, lazily fell into the west, and sunk deep into the horizon without the Man so much as noticing. With his meal held high, throat slick from lizard juices, and blanket wrapped around his shoulders, the Man walked long into the night humming songs of his youth, songs he'd sung to Marvin so that he'd heat meals so hot that peeling back the clear plastic sheets would send his fingers flying into his mouth to cool the steam-burnt skin, but his stomach growled inside of him, vibrating through his bones until his shoulders shook. Yet, with the life stolen from the hordes of reptiles, he dug his fist deep into his hairy belly and shouted, "Will you be quiet! Can't you wait? Soon, soon. I'll fill you soon enough. Your bellowing won't make the land any smaller. So, be silent!"

For hours, his shrinking gut obliged, but the constant pace and the blistering sun sent waves of insolence into his skin and his digestive sack took up its call again; his tired limbs, hearing the deafening grumbles, were swayed by its passion, and formed an internal sit-in, weighing each step down with the force of the fiery orb in the sky. Soon, his feet stopped lifting out of the sand, settling for dragging along the gritty landscape, bringing showers of dirt along for each labored movement. Each step, each lung-crushing moment, under the blistering sun weighed him down like heated stones piled along his shoulders until he was stooped over, walking on threes like a monkey. His breath huffed out of him in dry, bubbling waves until his feet would go no more, and his body toppled over into a mental darkness, which blackened all his senses save one and with that fading sense of touch, he felt something slightly cold and wet against his chest.

———◆———

"Come on, Marvin!" the Man said over the whir of his exercise bike. From his seat, wedging his ratty underwear between his ass cheeks, he looked at the soft yellow glow growing and shrinking with the speed of his pedaling feet. Though he knew he sweated from the cycling, he often pretended that Marvin's loving light warmed him out of love, and today was no different. The man watched his dinner of mashed

potatoes and braised beef spin on the glass tray, spotting the thin wisps of steam leaking out of the plastic sheet. He pedaled harder, hunching over the handle bar that could steer him nowhere, and then the sweet sound of Marvin's timer bell dinged into his ears, sending him rocketing off the bike, nearly tangling himself in the wires that crept up the ceiling like ivies. Kicking them off his toes, he struggled with the wires but turned to Marvin amidst his hopping, "I'll be right with you Marvin. Keep it warm for me," he laughed as he returned to his bindings.

"Marvin… what a pretty name for a pretty machine," a froggish voice croaked.

He tried to shriek in horror, but the chill in his blood tethered his limbs to a freakish halt. Ploombana the Brutal, the Man thought, knowing the protruding belly stretched the warlord's tight green military uniform with its glittering medals clinking like chains over his tiny heart. As soon as his small shoulders passed the doorway, Ploombana the Brutal's soldiers stormed in with their stolen leather boots and mismatched guns. One cracked the butt of his rifle against the Man's head, dropping him into a tangled marionette tied and bound by the wires that gave Marvin life. The pig-faced warlord tapped his sausage fingers against his many chin and bent to look at Marvin.

The Man screamed before a rifle-butt struck the side of his head, which was consumed with a sight-stealing pain that he felt down in the base of his testicles.

Ploombana the Brutal's chubby fingers opened the plastic door the same way he'd snatched the shirts off the backs of many abducted village girls. His upturned nose twitched on his face, letting the sweet smell of beef saturate the room. "Too good to eat, I say," the fat warlord chuckled. His men agreed with him three times in loud shouts, each one soothing Ploombana's eyes shut as if they stroked more than just his ego. He opened Marvin's door, taking the dinner out roughly. He brought the steaming plate close to his portly face and cooed, "Mmm… much too good to eat." Ploombana the Brutal turned the plate over, tapping its bottom like a disobedient child. The brown gravy fell into Marvin with clumps of buttered mashed potatoes; the Man watched as the contents poured out as if with no end. Marvin ate in loud plops under the endless faucet until mashed potatoes and gravy spilled out of the microwave's open mouth.

Ploombana the Brutal looked into the mess inside the microwave giggling. His plump fingers unhitched his belt, then his pants, before pushing them down past his lumpy calves. The Man screamed again as Ploombana the Brutal, his half-erect cock lolling about the coarse, matted pubic hair, took Marvin off the counter and eased its open face, the gravy mess spilling on the floor, onto his erection.

A rifle showered the Man's eyes with a wave of dancing stars, taking the colors of the world and warping them to a reality where blue was green and brown was yellow.

The sight of Ploombana the Brutal forcing himself into the mashed food and thrusting as deeply as he could sent the Man into a gagging fit of tears. The fat warlord tore into the microwave madly, rattling the door on its tiny hinges until the plastic seemed to scream and turning the dials as though he were groping a pair of fresh breasts. His bulbous face, slick with sweat, turned to his watching men and grunted, "Now! Poke him with pointy sticks!"

The men slung their weapons and tore at the walls as their leader slowly dipped his hips and thrusted again. Each soldier broke the thin sticks off the hut walls and prodded the Man; the tiny spears dug into him, twisting in his body hair and yanking them out in tiny explosions of stinging pain. He cried, but still they prodded and Ploombana the Brutal did not stop until a shudder of ejaculation blitzed through him, rippling along his blotched skin. His gut and buttocks continued to jiggle long afterwards like the aftershocks of an earthquake.

Marvin dripped onto the floor. The Man screamed his name.

———◆———

"Marvin!" the Man cried as he sprang up, scaring a flock of nibbling vultures that tore at his legs and sides and arms. One of the blonde, hunched birds shrieked as his hairy fist cracked its cowl of feathers, snapping the hollow bones easily. With flapping wings, the other stinking birds rose in a sickly children's circle away from the cursing man, sightless from delirium, whose hand shot from side to side with long strings of sandy foam. "Marvin!" he bellowed. The broken buzzard hopped into the air, but neither its wings nor the winds would take it up. The Man looked to the rolling sands but saw only the dream. In the space between them, he heard a shrill call for attention. It morphed into a croaking laugh as the wind kicked up sand into his face. He thought of the mix of mashed potatoes and semen oozing out of his beloved Marvin.

The Man gnashed his teeth with a sick grin that turned up towards his pupil-less eyes and his shoulders heaved like a busted kiddie pool. The vulture vomited at him, flapping its wings with its hooked beak and sharpened talons springing wildly. He took up his blanket and charged at the bird. With a trapper's skill born out of hate, the Man netted the thrashing creature in the blanket. Its black beak tore holes into the blue fabric and its claws, stuck in the fibers, struggled. Laughing, he looked for the largest stone in sight, settled for the nearest, and swung the makeshift sack high over his shoulder to bring it to a stop that sounded like a wet bundle of sticks cracking all at once. He brought the bag up again; nothing struggled. The dying bird stained the stone with spots of quickly drying blood. With the flick of his wrist, he unfolded the blanket, dropping the twisted pile of rot-fed meat and feathers.

The Man lifted the bird, parted the feathers, and sank into its shredded breast. He tore out strips and chomped on them until the shattered bones were ground fine enough to swallow. Crucified to the sun, the buzzard was a hollow shell that the Man ravenously attacked. The flesh tasted of rot bathed for days in urine, but still he ate. Despite himself, he ate.

Despite the indifferent look of his frozen meal, he ate.

Angry at his own weakness, the Man plucked the feathers off the bird husk by the fistful, scattering the floating things like a madman who wouldn't even watch as the dirty feathers flew away from him. The Man took up the bald bird by the bends of the wings and pulled at them. With a seething groan mixed with chest-heaving huffs, he tore the bird in two. In one hand, he held a limp wing and shoulder and the rest of the carrion bird in the other. He stood and spun, flinging the chunks to the dirt. Slowly, the sands buried the vulture with millions of floating grains piling against its broken body; soon, he wouldn't even know if it was all real or not, the only evidence rotting in his stomach.

Sucking the meat from the gaps in his teeth, the Man lifted the sandy frozen dinner and wept. With breath riddled with bloody spit, he blew the sand out of the plastic cookware and stared at it. "I couldn't wait. You saw me.

I didn't know what I was doing. I was in a dream. I didn't mean to," the Man blubbered. Wrapping his blanket around his warming head, the Man started way from the half-buried sin. He kissed the corner of the plate, then crushed it to his chest until the muscles in his arms groaned and shook. "Can you ever forgive me?" the Man asked his meal.

It remained silent.

———◆———

The Man walked with the chicken curry over his head during the long, hot days to thaw his meal and walked with it close to his sun-burnt chest at night to helplessly feel it freeze again.

———◆———

The Man's lips were flaky white like the scales of a shedding snake except the skin underneath the flakes weren't pretty and new; it was red and raw and stung whenever the constant wind slithered under the creases to bite at the sensitive flesh. The sound of lapping waves tangled in his matted hair and his half-closed eyes, yellow and tired, cared little for what was over the next dune, yet his burnt feet still moved him over it. At the top, his sunbaked eyes didn't immediately understand why the rest of the desert was moving, or why it was blue. By degrees, the smell of the water and the waves crashing against the shore brought smile to his face.

"Look," the Man called up to his meal, pointing near the shoreline: a massive ship crowded his vision of the vast emptiness of the ocean. It was low in the water with tiny boats milling around it. Sailors in unrecognizable uniforms called to each other and the wind dissected their words, flinging pieces of them at the Man. He smiled at the broken sounds of voices and took one step over the top of the dune only to fall. With his food slapped to his chest and blanket secured to his head, the Man rolled to the bottom of the sandy hill and, though he landed with his eyes looking up at the sun, all the Man saw was darkness.

———•———

He heard shouts and splashes, then lost consciousness again.

———•———

His eyes fluttered open, rocked awake by the matronly sway of the blue seas. He could see nothing, but he breathed easier. Fingers tried to pull the food away from him, and he struck the arm as hard as he could. He heard a splash, then half a dozen voices rose in a fit of panic and frustration.

———•———

"The Man won't open his arms, the silly sod," a voice chuckled.
"Ay, just use the blanket, and be glad you don't have to get your hands near his feet," another retorted. "I can't tell if they're dirty or just rotting off."

Like a soft, bloodstained hammock, his shoulders were lifted by the now taught blanket. He felt himself being hefted off the cold, moving ground. The shuffle of leather boots on steel whispered him to wake further, but the sound of the blanket tearing met the surrounding ears faster than his grumbling words. His top half fell; the back of his skull clunked against some unforgiving metal.

"Ah, pull him by the armpits then," one said.

"His armpits! You're a fucking cunt, you know that, Cecil?" the other said, then the Man heard nothing.

———•———

He dreamt of Ploombana the Brutal coming inside Marvin as if his testicles connected to an inexhaustible ocean of semen and woke screaming. "Where is it? Where is it!" the Man roared, his hands searching the space around him. He was wrapped in blankets, one of which was his tattered blue one, still gritty from the desert. The Man kicked the itchy naval sheets off of him and dropped to the cold metal floor but was up in an instant, wrapping his blue blanker tightly against him. His bare feet slapped the floor quickly and though he had no idea where he was or why the halls were bland and cold and cramped, he ran down them screaming for his food. Through all the twists and turns, he found one door ajar and when he slapped it open, the scent of chicken curry wafted like a heavy perfume into his nose.

A uniformed sailor, his hair shaved close to the sides of his head, looked up from his food, but still ate a forkful. "Awake, are you? About damn time, if you ask me."

The Man's hands tried to choke him from across the room and, though he slowly advanced, the sailor went back to his meal. "That stuff you had is in the freezer, if you're looking for it," he said, pointing beside the wild-eyed foreigner with a bent fork.

The Man tore open the old freezer door and in a mist of skin-curling cold, his meal sat clean and crystalline. He lifted it out gently, kissing its rim, and turned to the sailor with moist eyes. The sailor responded by silently pointing his fork at the tiny microwave set in the corner. The man ran to it, slid his meal inside, and his shaky fingers hung in the air, unsure of how to proceed. "It was about three minutes for mine. Doubt yours is any different," the sailor said as others entered whispering and motioning with their chins and eyes. But the only sounds the Man heard were the punched-in dings and the glowing hum of the beautiful machine.

On his knees, the Man watched the tray spin and the ice melt into a slush that warmed to savory gravy that spread over the frozen contents inside the magical device. The scent seeped from the gaps of the plastic door, and the Man's big shoulders bounced as he giggled and pressed his clammy fingers to the warm door. The numbers wound down as slow as his steps were in the sands he'd thankfully left behind, but soon the great chime of a fully cooked meal shot from his ears into his bones and out again.

"I wonder how it's going to taste," the Man heard the sailors say before every thought fell into his meal.

—ETC.—

Acknowledgments

"Jesus of Green Grit County, Texas" and "The Hungry Man Sees Far" were published by *Collective Exile: A Literary Magazine*.

"Small Truths" was published by *Nothing. No One. Nowhere.*

"The Rapist of Perversion Park" was published by *left hand of the father*.

The author would also like to acknowledge Christopher Amaya, the editor of this collection, and Ana Clamont, the artist responsible for the collection's cover.

ABOUT THE AUTHOR

Mario E. Martinez draws his inspiration from the landscape of the South Texas border. Where he lives, there is a constant clash between cultures, languages, religions, and ideologies. It is at once modern and traditional, a place where busy roads cut through ranchlands heavy with cattle, where the dark mysteries of the natural world sit beside shopping plazas and newly built neighborhoods. His other works, *Twin Burials* and *San Casimiro, Texas: Short Stories*, were published through AuthorHouse.